"Looks clear," Ree whispered. "Ready?"

Quint shook his head. "You go. I'll stay here, keep watch and provide cover."

"Okay," she said, not wasting a second—or maybe just not giving him a minute to rethink the offer. Quint pulled his gun from his holster, ready to fire if need be.

He watched Ree's dark silhouette as she moved across the parking lot with ease. She zigzagged back and forth before crouching low to drop a listening device. After moving to a second location in much the same manner, she made her way back. Trusting her had been the right move.

After holstering his weapon, he hopped up in one fluid motion and led them back toward his truck. They made a wide circle, coming at the vehicle from the opposite side of the street. The second they cleared the last building, Quint froze.

There were two guys around his truck...

NEWLYWED ASSIGNMENT

USA TODAY Bestselling Author

BARB HAN

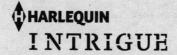

HARLEQUIN

INTRIGUE

All my love to Brandon, Jacob and Tori, the three great loves
of my life.

To Babe, my hero, for being my best friend, my greatest love
and my place to call home.

I love you all with everything that I am.

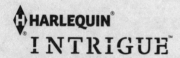

ISBN-13: 978-1-335-48963-0

Recycling programs
for this product may
not exist in your area.

Newlywed Assignment

Copyright © 2022 by Barb Han

For questions and comments about the quality of this book,
please contact us at CustomerService@Harlequin.com.

Harlequin Enterprises ULC
22 Adelaide St. West, 41st Floor
Toronto, Ontario M5H 4E3, Canada
www.Harlequin.com

Printed in U.S.A.

USA TODAY bestselling author Barb Han lives in north Texas with her very own hero-worthy husband, three beautiful children, a spunky golden retriever/ standard poodle mix and too many books in her to-read pile. In her downtime, she plays video games and spends much of her time on or around a basketball court. She loves interacting with readers and is grateful for their support. You can reach her at barbhan.com.

Books by Barb Han

Harlequin Intrigue

A Ree and Quint Novel

Undercover Couple
Newlywed Assignment

An O'Connor Family Mystery

Texas Kidnapping
Texas Target
Texas Law
Texas Baby Conspiracy
Texas Stalker
Texas Abduction

Rushing Creek Crime Spree

Cornered at Christmas
Ransom at Christmas
Ambushed at Christmas
What She Did
What She Knew
What She Saw

Decoding a Criminal

Visit the Author Profile page at Harlequin.com.

CAST OF CHARACTERS

Emmaline Ree Sheppard, aka Ree—This ATF agent will do anything to protect a partner who refuses to save himself.

Quinton Casey, aka Quint—This hotshot ATF agent blames himself for his partner Tessa's death and will stop at nothing to put the person responsible behind bars, placing himself in danger in the process.

Lola—This bartender is the key to get closer to one of Dumitru's men.

Esteban—This brother is in deep with a bad crowd.

Matias—Who is the father of Lola's child really and what does he know?

Constantin—Lola's boyfriend runs a shipping business, but is that all?

Dumitru—The ultimate target and person responsible for Tessa's murder is elusive—too much so?

Chapter One

Why did every backyard barbecue with Emmaline Ree Sheppard's family turn into a not-so-subtle hint that she was failing her mother? At thirty-six years old, Ree wasn't married. She had no immediate plans to have a family. And she didn't bake anything from scratch.

Sue her.

Ree did, however, have a job as an undercover agent for the ATF that she loved, a great house that she'd bought with her own money, and a fulfilling dating life. To be honest, two out of three of those things were true, but not having a man in her life wasn't a problem for her, so it shouldn't bother anyone else, either.

"Do you want to go inside and clean yourself up before the food is ready?" her mother asked. The woman was five feet two inches of pure spit and vinegar.

"I showered this morning," Ree said more than a little defensively. What now? She didn't know how to shower properly?

"You could do something with your hair," her mother continued, undaunted.

"It's fine," Ree said as the others quieted. Everyone but Mother seemed to hear the caution in those words.

"While you're inside, you can put up whatever's in that bag," Mother said, wrinkling her nose.

"Do you mean cheesecake?" Ree asked, her pulse rising faster than the Texas heat.

"Evelyn baked, so we'll save yours for later," Mother said with a flick of her wrist, referring to Ree's sister-in-law.

The way Ree saw it, she had two choices. Let her tongue rip and probably say things she would regret or march inside with her store-bought cheesecake that her mother had already insulted and cool off in the air conditioning.

Her mother opened her mouth to speak, so Ree put a hand up to stop her. "I just can't do this right now, Mother."

Frustration seethed as she stormed toward the house and into the kitchen with her brother on her heels. Hot tears threatened, but she refused to let them fall.

"I'm sorry if I wasn't the kind of girl who wore frilly dresses and big bows in my hair," Ree said to her oldest brother, Shane, with a little more heat than she'd intended. She smacked her flat palm against the kitchen counter of her mother's ranch-style house.

"She doesn't mean it like that, Ree," Shane defended. She'd gone by the nickname Ree for as long as she could remember.

"Oh, really? How am I supposed to take a comment like that?" she countered. "And what's wrong with my hair anyway?"

"Nothing. You look fine. And for the record, you would look beautiful no matter what you did with your hair. All I'm saying is that you might be taking every comment she makes to heart." He put his hands in the air, palms out in the surrender position, when Ree shot him *the look*.

"She went straight from my hair to attacking my store-bought cheesecake," she continued, holding up the box. "We all know I don't cook."

"Bake," he corrected.

Wrong move, Shane.

"Are you kidding me right now?" she asked.

"I still don't think she meant it so harshly," he said with a look of compassion.

"Fine." She circled the small room. "Tell me how I should react."

"You could crack a joke, for one," he started.

"She would love that coming from me," she countered. "Because Mom has always had one amazing sense of humor when it comes to her only daughter."

"She laughs at my jokes," he stated, sounding more than a little defensive.

"Case in point," Ree said on a sharp sigh. Her brother had no idea what it was like *not* to be their mother's favorite. He couldn't help himself. She also acknowledged he was trying to calm her down out of love.

Shane cocked his head to one side and studied her like she was part of a final exam and he was about to fail the class. "Are you sure this is about her?"

"Yes," she quickly countered. Too quickly? "Who else riles me up like our dear old mother?"

"You shouldn't refer to her like that," he said, shaking his head.

She resisted the urge to tell him that she had a pretty good handle on what she should and shouldn't do because when she dialed down her frustration, she could acknowledge he was right. Ree was all defense right now when she should probably figure out a way to calm down. She'd been on edge since her most recent undercover case ended a few days ago. Her partner, Agent Quinton Casey, aka Quint, had left quite an impression on her. They'd shared a sizzling kiss that had replayed in her dreams more than once in the past few nights. Quint was most likely onto a new case by now. One that worried her because of its connection to the death of his best friend and former partner.

"She sure knows how to push my buttons," she defended, gripping the edge of the counter so hard her knuckles turned white.

"Don't take this the wrong way, but I'm pretty sure the feeling is mutual," he said.

"Not you, too," she said.

"What?"

"Hopping on the 'Mom bandwagon' and making me feel bad for having words with her," she continued. This discussion should have been over before it started. Ree was having a moment and wasn't ready to let her frustration go. Why was that? It wasn't like her to hang on to hurt. An annoying voice in the back of her mind pointed out she was always defensive when it came to her mother. Was it true?

The creak of the screen door opening in the adjacent room broke into the moment. Ree walked over to the fridge, then shifted a couple of cartons around to make room for her store-bought cheesecake. Forget that it had been her mother's favorite and most requested at birthdays. Shane's wife had baked sourdough bread, and French macarons with raspberry-rose buttercream. Evelyn loved to bake, and Ree planned to eat both. But it needed to be okay that Ree wasn't into the same things. Wasn't variety the spice of life anyway?

Shane disappeared into the living room as she flexed and released her fingers a couple of times in an attempt to work off some of the tension. This was the reason she'd stopped coming to Sunday suppers. She didn't enjoy the stress that came from interactions with her mother, and it just became easier to stay away than to face another letdown.

As Ree took in a slow breath, she heard her ex-boyfriend's voice in the next room. Preston was Shane's best friend, so it wasn't out of the norm for him to show up at a barbecue. So why was she suddenly not all that happy at the prospect of seeing him?

"Hey," Preston said as he walked into the kitchen. He was six feet one with a runner's build. He had light blue eyes and sandy-blond hair. He had a one-inch scar on his left cheek that she used to think was sexy, and would be considered good-looking by most standards. Women lit up when he entered a room. Shouldn't she do the same?

"Hi, Preston. It's good to see you," she said, and tried to mean it.

He walked over to her, and then leaned forward for

a kiss. She turned at the last moment, offering a cheek instead. He planted one on her, but it was the most awkward thing. She mumbled an apology and took a step back.

"How have you been?" she asked, pretending that didn't just happen.

"Good," he said, taking her in with his gaze. "How's work?"

"Same. Good," she parroted, realizing this shouldn't be such an awkward exchange. The two of them might have dated at one time, but those feelings were long over. She'd considered reconnecting with him for a second while on her last assignment, but she was thinking clearly now. A voice in the back of her mind said she'd needed a diversion from the out-of-place attraction she'd felt for her partner. Quint was the opposite of Preston in just about every conceivable way, but a workplace romance could be a career killer.

"I'm just going to check on the kids," Shane said, not making eye contact as he made a beeline for the back door.

Great. He was leaving her alone with Preston. *Way to go, Shane. And thanks for the support.*

"Yeah, so, maybe we should join them?" she asked as her brother practically bolted out of the kitchen.

"Or we could stay in here and talk," Preston offered.

"Okay," she said for lack of anything better. Besides, facing down her mother while Ree was still riled up probably wasn't the best move.

Preston motioned toward the small table in the eat-in kitchen. "How about iced tea or lemonade?"

"Sure. Go ahead," she said. "I think I'll have a beer." Her thoughts immediately drifted to the way she'd left things with Quint. She'd asked him to call if he ever wanted to get together for a beer. As expected, her phone had been silent. There was no way he would pass up the opportunity to chase Tessa's killer.

"This early?" His eyebrow shot up.

"Day off," she said by way of explanation, but in truth she was just trying to get through this gathering. She moved to the fridge and then grabbed a cold one. Where was her grandfather? He would definitely join her in a beer despite the fact that it was the middle of the afternoon. She was such an inexperienced drinker she'd be taking a nap in an hour. Then there'd be a headache. But it would be almost worth it to see her mother's disapproval again. At least this time she'd have a reason to be disappointed in her daughter. "You know what? Never mind. I think I'll put on a pot of coffee instead. Want a cup?"

Preston shook his head. His expression said it was unthinkable to drink coffee in this Texas summer heat.

She would have a Coke if there was any. Her mother had a couple of rules. No guns. No soda. No fun. Okay, Ree added the last part on her own.

"So, how many days off do you have?" Preston asked.

"A couple," she said. "I just got off an intense assignment so…"

She stopped right there when his nose wrinkled and his face puckered like he'd just sucked on a pickled prune.

"What?" she asked, even though she should know better at this point. Work talk was off-limits with Preston.

The back door opened and her mother walked in, saving Ree from the conversation sure to come after Preston's expression morphed to frustrated. The same old song and dance that Ree was in a dangerous job and should look for something with a desk attached to it.

"Oh, Preston, I didn't realize you were coming today," her mother said.

Really? Because Ree was 100 percent certain her mother *did* know he was invited.

"I'm here," he said, walking over and giving her mother a peck on the cheek.

"Ree, would you mind bringing out some ice?" Mother asked.

"Not at all," she said, noticing her mother never once glanced in Ree's direction. She was being silly. She was a grown woman, a successful woman, and her mother's disapproval shouldn't hurt so much. "I'll be right out."

"Thanks," Mother said before motioning toward Preston. "And make our guest feel at home."

Wow. Was she not?

"Okay, Mom. I'll make sure Preston puts his feet on the furniture and walks around in his underwear," she quipped.

Mother's disapproval was written all over her face before she seemed to shake it off and put on a forced smile. At least Ree had given the woman a reason to be upset this time.

"I'll be outside," Mother announced, nose in the air.

Maybe Ree shouldn't have poked the bear. Shane probably had a point. Ree was most likely making the situation worse with her attitude. She would apologize later and do her best to smooth things over. She would also stand her ground. Just because her father was killed in the line of duty almost twenty-five years ago didn't mean the same would happen to Ree. Agencies were even more cautious now, and agents were better trained. Mistakes happened like with any other job. Those mistakes sometimes resulted in a fatality. It was a terrible reality in this line of work. Ree had no intention of becoming one of those statistics.

The sound of gravel spewing underneath tires caused her heart to skip a few beats.

"I haven't seen my grandfather in so long. I gotta go." Ree wasted no time rushing to the front door.

The truck speeding toward her didn't belong to her grandfather, that was for sure. As she stepped onto the porch, she got a good look at the driver. What was Quint Casey doing here?

QUINT HAD NO idea if he was about to be asked to turn tail and head back from where he came or if he would be welcomed with open arms. Based on the fact that Ree had come out the front door and was heading toward him, he wasn't going to have to wait long to find out.

He parked behind a slew of vehicles. Clearly, there was some kind of family gathering going on. Sunday supper? Hadn't Ree mentioned something about this being a ritual?

Seeing her again caused his chest to squeeze and a knot to form in his gut. She looked good standing there, leaning against a convertible, all long legs, red hair and emerald eyes. Their last kiss came to mind, causing his pulse to jump up a few notches. Did the vehicle belong to her? Because for one quick moment, he could see her behind the wheel on a sunny day with her hair in the wind.

Arms crossed over her chest, toe tapping, a look of curiosity stamped her features.

He exited his truck and walked toward her as a guy took two steps out the front door, stopping on the porch.

"You're about the last person I thought I'd see here," Ree said with a smirk.

"Boyfriend?" He nodded toward the guy behind her, standing far enough away not to be able to hear their conversation.

"No. Friend." Her smile faded, her gaze narrowed and her chin jutted out in a way that made him realize she was defensive on this subject.

"Is there a place we can go to talk?" He'd come all this way. He might as well go for broke.

"Why are you here?" she asked, not budging.

"To see you," he said with a wink. Stating the obvious no matter how funny he tried to be with it didn't seem to impress her much. His attempt to lighten the mood fell flat. "In all seriousness, I'd like a word if you can spare fifteen minutes of your time."

"Everything okay, Ree?" her friend asked, but his voice wasn't filled with a whole lot of confidence.

Quint gave her a look.

"His name is Preston," she said, looking annoyed.

Quint would give it to the man. He was attempting the whole knight-in-shining-armor routine. The move signaled how much the guy cared about Ree. Most folks would walk the other way when confronted with a person of Quint's size and general demeanor. He knew he didn't exactly give off a friendly vibe when he didn't need to for a case.

"Ree?" Preston said a little louder this time.

"All good," she said, sounding more frustrated than anything else. "It's work-related."

"At Sunday supper?" Preston asked with disdain in his tone.

Quint folded his arms across his chest, figuring this conversation was about to become real interesting based on the sparks in her eyes.

"Mind if we talk about this later, Preston?" she countered. "I need to speak to Quint alone."

"This the guy from your last case?" Preston didn't seem to realize this wasn't the time to dig his heels in.

"You know I don't discuss the details of my work," she said without looking back. She kept her gaze focused on Quint, almost daring him to say something.

He figured this wasn't the time to take the bait. Her shoulders were locked up and there was more tension radiating from her than gunfire at a shooting range.

"But at the ranch?" Preston didn't seem to know when to stop.

Quint wiggled his eyebrows at Ree. The move was probably not smart. And yet he couldn't seem to stop himself.

Ree's face broke into a wide smile. She mouthed the word *jerk*. Then she turned around and walked over to Preston. Whatever she said to him worked, because he touched her on the shoulder before turning around and heading inside.

When she whirled around on Quint, all the humor was gone from her face. "What do you really want?"

"You," he started, but she cut him off with a look.

"What if I'm not an option?" she asked, stopping a foot in front of him. She mimicked his body language, folding her arms across her chest as she jutted her chin out again.

"We worked well together before," he stated.

"I'm honored you would want me back, but—"

"You haven't heard the details yet," he continued.

"Don't need to," she argued. "You're going after the jerk you think is responsible for Tessa's death. Aren't you?"

"All I'm doing is following the evidence from our last case. And like it or not, we make a good team. We already have an established cover story. It's less work to—"

"Oh, so you're saying you don't really want me. You just want someone easy." She drew out the last word.

"Not what I meant at all," he countered.

"Yes it is," she said, poking him in the chest with her index finger. "It's exactly what you said."

"Okay. How about this?" he started, figuring he needed a new tactic. "I miss working with you."

Ree rolled her eyes.

"You're going to have to try harder than that," she

said. "Actually, never mind. You need to dial it down a few notches."

This was exactly the fire and sass he'd missed over the past couple of days. Not that he would admit it publicly.

"You're a good agent. I need someone who can step right in and work beside me without getting in the way," he stated as honestly as he could.

"I can't do it, and we both know why," she challenged.

"Do we?" he asked. She gave away nothing in her eyes as to whether or not he was making any headway with her.

"You could just pull rank and get me assigned," she said. "Why come here and ask in person?"

"Because you're the best damn agent I've worked with in a long time. I don't want anyone else by my side on this case. And you know how to hold your own," he said. "If none of that convinces you, I'll add that I think we make a good team."

Again, he was having a difficult time reading her as she stood there. At least she hadn't delivered a hard no.

"I can't read your mind." He finally broke the silence. "Any chance you'll consider it?"

"Not a good idea, Quint" was all she said before turning to walk away.

He couldn't leave without a reason, so he followed her.

Chapter Two

"Hold on."

Ree stopped, but she didn't turn around as Quint's masculine voice traveled over her and through her. They had barely closed the books on their last case, where they'd brought down a money laundering scheme being run out of a combination restaurant and bar. They'd learned the person Quint was truly after, a guy by the name Dumitru, was farther up the chain and much harder to reach. Going undercover with Quint while he was on a witch hunt wasn't her idea of smart.

Then again, she worried about him bringing in a brand-new partner after the two of them had developed good working chemistry. Their recent undercover sting had been akin to baptism by fire, but she'd learned a great deal from the ATF's most seasoned agent. They had chemistry to burn, but that definitely fell into the "cons" column.

At six feet three inches of stacked muscle, stormy sapphire-blue eyes and strong chin with just the right amount of stubble, Quint Casey would be considered sexy by most standards. His muscled torso formed an improbable vee at the waist, and he had the kind of body most athletic recruiters would have killed for. He had the whole "chiseled jawline, strong, hawklike nose and piercing eyes" bit down pat.

"I can admit that I'm not the easiest person to get along with at times. Is there any way you would consider taking on another undercover case with me?" he asked with eyes that locked onto hers, causing more heat and electricity to fire through her. "We have to move fast on the information we have, and I can't think of a better partner."

"Are you sure about that?" She was starting to waver despite the warning bells sounding off in her head. Their chemistry had felt special and not easy to duplicate. "Because there are other agents who would give their right arm to work with you."

"I'm one hundred percent," he said with full conviction as he studied her. "Can I ask a question?"

"Go for it," she said, figuring she might as well hear what he had to say. The least she could do was listen after he'd made the long trip to her mother's ranch. Plus, she could admit part of her would rather be out here talking shop with Quint than doing the family supper bit. It was getting harder to feel like she fit in anymore, especially since her grandfather seemed to be a no-show.

"What's *really* holding you back?" he asked.

"Are you sure you want to know?" She didn't bother to hide her shock at his question.

"I can handle whatever it is," he said. "Trust me."

Famous last words, she thought. But if he really wanted to know...

"The personal stakes are high for you, and I'm concerned mistakes could end up being made because of it." There. She'd said it. Tessa had been killed by accident while Quint was trying to bust a weapons ring that went by the name A12. Dumitru was the leader and he'd been present at the bust. He was also the only one who got away that night. The others who'd been busted ended up dead in their jail cells.

"That's understandable," he said after a thoughtful pause. A look passed behind his eyes, nothing more than a flash, really, that said she'd struck a nerve.

"There's a reason lawyers aren't allowed to try cases for family members," she continued.

"Conflict of interest," he stated.

"As much as I hate to say it, because I do realize you're the best person we have at the agency," she continued, doing what she could to soften the blow. "But even you can't deny how tempting it would be to follow a lead when we should stay back and analyze if you feel like you're close to the person responsible for Tessa's death."

Quint nodded, his expression unreadable.

After a few uncomfortable beats of silence, he turned around and walked toward the driver's side of his truck.

"Quint," she said, but he kept walking. She ran over to him and placed her hand on his shoulder. "Talk to me."

"What's the point?" He opened the door and claimed the driver's seat.

"I don't know. This is how people work things out." She wedged her body so he couldn't close the door without hurting her. The irony that she hadn't discussed her feelings with her mother, yet she was forcing him to talk, sat heavy on her chest. Why was it so easy to dish out advice and so difficult to take it?

"Your mind is made up," he said, reaching for the handle. "There's basically no point in continuing this conversation. Don't worry, I won't request you for this assignment."

"Wait. Wait. Wait," she said. "What do you mean you won't request me? I thought it was already a done deal."

"No. That's why I came here to talk to you in person," he stated. "And the fact that you think I would go behind your back only proves I didn't know you as well as I believed."

"I just thought—"

"What? That I'd make arrangements without consulting you first?" His look of frustration was a nail in her gut. "If you'll move out of the way, I'll get going. I've taken up enough of your time." He nodded toward the backyard. "Your family is waiting. You should get back to them."

Ree stood there, dumbfounded. Words tried to form, but her mouth wouldn't move. Since she couldn't speak, she decided to act. She stepped up and slipped into the back seat.

"What are you doing?" he asked, craning his neck around.

She shrugged and put her hands up, palms out, in the surrender position.

"I'm trying to leave," he said.

"Then you'll have to take me with you." She finally found her voice. The thought of Quint tackling this assignment with a new partner, one he barely knew, wasn't something Ree was willing to allow. Granted, he was a professional and at the top of his game. Did he make mistakes? Yes. Everyone did. She'd made several that he hadn't held against her.

"Does this mean you're trying to weasel your way back into my good graces?" Quint quipped.

"We'll see about that when you hear what I have to say next," she said.

"Sounds like I should be very afraid," he stated, his tone a little lighter now. The stress wrinkle on his forehead was near-permanent.

"I need a minute to think about what you're asking before I make a decision," she started. "So that means you get to spend the day with my family if you want me to consider taking the assignment."

"It would be easier for me to call upstairs and make the request," he said as his gaze found hers via the rearview mirror.

"Yeah. That's true." She nodded. "But you won't do that."

"And why is that?" he asked, arching a dark brow.

"Easy," she said. "You want me to show up willingly and in a good mood. Force me and we both know I'll have an attitude."

"I have seen your temper," he agreed with a smirk. One that caused her stomach to free-fall. Her attraction to him definitely fell into the *con* column. One very solid *pro* was his experience. The idea of working with him again was growing on her. A small part of her wished he'd called for that beer instead. But dating a coworker was probably a bad idea. "Fortunately for you, I don't scare easily."

"Sounds like I'm one lucky lady." She twisted up her face as she rolled her eyes.

"That's a fair statement," he quipped.

Ree sighed. They'd used their simmering attraction to sell the newlywed routine on their previous assignment. She'd been tempted to cross a line with him more than once in the cabin they'd shared on the last bust. At least she'd be going into this case with eyes wide open.

Hold on a sec. Was she seriously considering taking the assignment?

"What do you say?" she asked. "My family is probably holding out on serving food. We'll have a small but angry mob soon if I don't get over there."

Quint stared at her for a long moment.

"I don't normally do family get-togethers, but I'll make an exception this time," he said. "Just don't think this is going to become a habit."

"As long as you remember that I haven't agreed to anything yet," she said.

Quint stepped out of the truck and then held his hand out. "You will."

"What makes you so certain?" She took the offering, ignoring the now-familiar jolt of electricity that came with contact. Her heart hoped she could take being in close quarters again with Quint.

"I'm going to charm the hell out of your family,"

he said. "I'll have them eating out of my hand by the time I'm through. You'll take the case just to get them off your back."

Ree laughed out loud as she dropped his hand.

"Yeah?" she asked with a raised eyebrow. "Good luck with that one."

The man had no idea what he was getting into.

QUINT HAD THIS. No problem. He could handle families despite the fact that he'd grown up the child of a single mother. How hard could it be? It wasn't like he was socially inept. He'd been to quite a few parties over the years. He'd done his fair share of socializing at department functions despite preferring a quiet night at home on his days off over spending time with a dozen people he barely knew. So why was a thin sheen of sweat forming above his eyebrows?

He'd spent the better part of the past ten years pretending to be someone else for a living. Surely he could put on the same mask and get through a couple of hours with these good people.

"Ready for this?" Ree asked before pinching the bridge of her nose and exhaling a long, slow sigh.

That was probably not a good sign.

"I've dealt with worse things than a family barbecue," he snapped. The words came out a little more heated than he'd intended. Why were his nerves getting to him?

Ree was important. He respected her work. It was natural for him to want her family to like him. Or so he tried to convince himself.

"Let the fireworks begin," she said so low he almost didn't hear her.

Ree led the way around the side of the house. A couple of kids were running around, blowing bubbles and hopping in and out of a small plastic pool filled with water from a garden hose that snaked over the edge.

The sun glared and for a half second, Quint almost doubled back to get his sunglasses. He decided against it at the last minute, figuring her family would want to look him in the eye.

There were a couple of wooden picnic tables underneath a towering oak tree. A miniature plastic table sat in between. Laughter filled the air as a slightly older woman with the same fiery red hair as Ree carried a basket to one of the tables. This whole scene was something out of a Norman Rockwell painting, and definitely out of his comfort zone. This seemed like a good time to remind himself he was doing this for Ree.

Instinct or habit had him reaching for her hand. He stopped himself midreach. They weren't playing the married couple right now, and based on the stare-down he was receiving, Preston fit into this family far better than Quint ever would.

"Hey, everyone, I'd like you to meet one of my co-workers." Ree clapped her hands together just in case no one got the message based on her booming voice—a voice that echoed across the several-acre lawn. Ree held her hand up like she was presenting an auction item. "Everyone, this is Agent Quinton Casey. Quint, this is everyone."

He suddenly felt like a bug underneath a magnifying glass on a hot summer sidewalk.

"Hey," he said, then gave an awkward wave that he was pretty sure made him look more like Howdy Doody than a top ATF agent.

Ree's mother gave a curt nod before turning to the other table with her basket. Preston's stare-down continued. Little did the guy know that with Quint's martial arts training he wasn't the guy Preston wanted to pick a fight with. Then again, Quint wasn't here to stir up trouble.

One guy stood up and walked over to the perimeter of the manicured lawn where Quint stood.

"I'm Shane, Ree's brother." He stuck a hand out in between them. "We've talked over the phone a couple of times."

"Nice to meet you in person." Quint took the offering and received a vigorous handshake.

"I'll just leave you two to get to know each other," Ree said with a half smirk before taking off toward a cooler. She grabbed two cold ones, popped open the tops and brought one back to Quint before making a beeline for the kids' table.

Ree with kids? He didn't think she was the type to hang around with the little rug rats on purpose.

"Do you want to come over and have a seat?" Shane asked. "I'd like to introduce you to my best friend, Preston."

"We've met," Quint said quickly. A little too quickly?

"Oh," Shane said, looking at a loss for words.

"But, hey, it can't hurt to get to know each other

better." Quint figured his attraction to Ree would cool down quite a few notches if he got to know the guy who had to be an ex-boyfriend.

"Great." Shane led the way over to the picnic table where Preston sat. He pointed to one of the men sitting beside Preston. "That's my brother Finn."

Finn glanced up and smiled. "Nice to meet you." He almost immediately went back to his conversation or hostile negotiation with a little tyke with the same shock of red hair.

"That would be my son Liam who is doing all the talking." Shane practically beamed with pride.

"Cute kid," Quint said. As far as kids went, this one would pass muster. He had a round, angelic face that was dotted with freckles.

"Thanks," Shane said. "Over at the other table are Patrick and Connor."

The two perked up when they heard their names. Both glanced over and waved before returning to animated conversation. The family resemblance among the Sheppards was unmistakable.

Shane took a seat beside Preston, so Quint took a spot opposite them both.

"How long have you known Ree?" Preston asked, gripping his plastic fork so hard it might crack.

"Not long," Quint admitted. "But I do feel like we got to know each other fast."

"Really?" Preston's eyebrow went up. "That's odd."

Shane made a face at his friend before saying, "Ree can be a closed book to most people."

"Nature of the job," Quint defended. "When your

life depends on selling the fact that you are newlyweds, barriers break down real fast."

Mrs. Sheppard gasped at hearing the last part. She clutched her chest with her free hand and took a step back.

"It's no big deal, Mom." Ree shot a look of apology at Quint.

He'd clearly overstepped his bounds. Duly noted.

"If you really knew Ree, you wouldn't talk about the dangers of work around her family," Preston said, low and under his breath.

Quint took in a slow, deep breath. Turned out he wasn't as good at this family thing as he'd expected.

Ree walked over to him, giving her brothers a death stare. She plopped down beside him, turning her back to the table.

"Do you want to get out of here?" she asked, and he could see her clench her back teeth.

"Is that a good idea?" He didn't want to make matters worse.

"It is as far as I'm concerned," she countered.

"You asked me to stay. It's up to you when I leave," he stated, and meant every word. Based on the chilly reception from her mother, a picture was emerging. Ree had touched on her family dynamic a little bit while they were on their last assignment, but seeing it first-hand put the reality of the situation smack in his face. He would unpack it all later. For now, he just wanted to do whatever it took to make Ree happy so she'd agree to the assignment.

"Let's get out of here," she said, pushing up to standing.

"Hey, Ree. Where are you going?" Shane asked.

"Somewhere people know how to treat a guest," she said.

With that, she marched around the side of the house. Quint followed, figuring his popularity with her family took another hit.

"I'll follow you in my car," she said.

"Where to?" he asked.

"Anywhere but here." Her voice shook with anger.

Footsteps sounded behind them. Quint turned to see Preston jogging up.

"Ree, don't leave like this," Preston said, stopping at the corner of the house.

"I have to prep for a case," she said by way of defense. She stopped next to her convertible with her hand on the door handle but didn't turn around.

Quint headed to his truck, figuring it wasn't his place to listen.

"Really? Are you choosing work again? Because you're going to turn around in a few years and realize you're all alone." Preston's voice held far too much disdain for his own good. The man seemed to have no idea the land mine he'd just stepped on. A person like Ree needed support, not more criticism. She was clearly taking enough from her mother. The last thing she needed was to hear it from someone she was in a relationship with. But Ree didn't need Quint to step up and defend her. She'd do a fine job on her own.

In fact, as he hopped into the driver's seat, he could practically hear all of Ree's muscles tensing at once.

He had no idea what her response ended up being. All he could hear was her tires searching for purchase on the dirt road before her vehicle whipped right past his.

Chapter Three

Ree pulled over to the side of the road and waved at Quint to pull beside her. She rarely lost her temper, but her last button had been pushed, and she refused to have the same argument with Preston that had ended every attempt to have a relationship. This was history repeating itself. She should have known better. Losing her temper was right up there with epic bad ideas, but she'd done it anyway. Then there was her mother to consider. Ree would have to circle back and make peace. She also made a mental note to skip Sundays at the ranch when this next case was behind her.

"My house is about a mile from here. Want to go there and have a cup of coffee?" she asked, figuring they could go over the details of the assignment there. Plus, she could pack.

"Lead the way" was all he said.

Her heart thundered at the thought of Quint in her personal space. She shook it off, focusing instead on the work ahead. Another assignment, this time even more dangerous. Not that she minded. All it made her realize was that she wanted to be that much more prepared. The recent Greenlight Restaurant and Bar sting had blown wide open faster than expected. This case might follow in its footsteps.

She wanted to be as prepared as possible. Although, to be fair, these operations took on a life of their own in the heat of the moment. All the preparation in the world couldn't stop unknowns from coming into play.

Ree parked on the pad beside her two-bedroom bungalow. She waved for Quint to park behind her car. There was no reason for him not to hem her in, considering the next time she left would likely be with him.

Rather than wait around for him, she walked to her front door and unlocked it. Leaving it open behind her, she set down her purse and keys on the console table lining the hallway. Coffee would help clear her mind after the encounter with her family. Preston had been a jerk to Quint, but that wasn't the main reason she felt so put out. Being on bad terms with her mother always put her on edge, and it seemed like there was nothing she could do to stop the woman from worrying.

A quick knock sounded from the next room before she heard Quint's boots shuffle across the tile floor.

"I'm in the kitchen" was all she said.

Having him in her home sent a thrill of awareness skittering across her skin. Awareness of his masculine presence. Awareness of his strength. Awareness of his spicy male scent as he stepped into her small kitchen. A file folder was tucked underneath his left arm. She figured it contained the details of their next assignment.

She made quick work of fixing two cups of coffee, handing one over as steam billowed.

"Thank you," he said before taking a sip. "Can't say it's better than the beer you handed me a while ago, but it certainly keeps the mind sharper."

She smiled at his offhanded remark as he winked.

"Let's have a seat at the table." She motioned toward the adjacent room that had a round table with two chairs, realizing her furniture was meant for regular-sized people and not those with the kind of height and rippled muscles on Quint.

He made it work, figuring out a way to fit and look comfortable in the process. But that was just Quint. He could make just about anything work and look good doing it.

After setting his coffee mug down, he placed the folder on top of the table. Using his index fingers, he pushed it to her side. This folder was something that could be bought at a corner drugstore.

"This doesn't look like a work file." She took a sip of fresh brew, enjoying the burn on her throat.

"Nope. It's personal."

"Information you've put together on your own?" she asked, not liking where this conversation was headed.

"Yes and no. I have gathered some of the intel from work." He shot a look because he must realize she could turn him in.

"What exactly are you getting me into, Quint?" she asked, wondering how many lines he'd be willing to cross if it meant catching the man responsible for Tessa's death. "What if we don't catch Dumitru this time?"

Quint stared at the rim of his coffee mug for a long moment. When he looked up, he said, "I'm going the distance on this one, Ree. You can decide what you want to do at any time. You're not locked in. If it gets uncomfortable, you can walk. No harm, no foul."

"Those sure are pretty words," she said right back. "We both know I won't walk away from an assignment and leave you vulnerable. If you're supposed to walk in there with a wife, I'm not going to ditch you when it gets rough."

"Fair enough." He gave a slight nod.

There was no way he would leave her stranded in the middle of a case, and he had to know the reverse was true.

"Let's see what's inside this file." She opened it. There was a rudimentary tree drawing with branches. Some had labels. Others didn't. At the top was Dumitru's name. At the bottom were the names she recognized from Greenlight. "So we don't know how many layers there are between Greenlight and Dumitru."

"No, we don't. All I can say for certain is this 'transportation' operation out of Houston is somehow linked to him." He used his fingers to make air quotes around the word *transportation.*

"Someone who owns a trucking company would have an easier time hauling weapons," she stated. "There's a whole lot of scrutiny on a business like that, though."

"You're not wrong," he said. "Which is why I don't believe they're as involved as it looks."

"A decoy?" she asked.

"Yes. They're owned by a shell corporation out of the Bahamas." He pointed to the name, Trux.

"I'm guessing Trux owns other businesses," she said.

"I'd like to find out if they do. We both know the challenge of tying shell corps to actual businesses," he said.

"Which is why the trucking operation is most likely real," she reasoned.

"It could lead us to greener pastures, and that's why I want to follow through with this investigation." He picked up his mug and took a sip.

"Okay, just please tell me I don't have to serve food to anyone else. I'd like to shelve my serving tray, if you know what I mean," she said on a sigh. Being a waitress at Greenlight had pushed her to the limits of good acting. Not to mention those double shifts that left her feet aching.

When he didn't speak, she mouthed the word *no* as she looked up at him.

"There's no food involved," he said with the kind of smile that probably broke a lot of hearts.

"Seriously?" she asked. "Again?"

"It's not my fault restaurants and bars are known hangouts of the kind of people we bust. If they hung out in churches, they probably wouldn't end up on our list in the first place," he defended.

"When are you going to be the one to parade around in clothes that leave far too little to the imagination?" she asked, and they both laughed.

"I could, but I doubt anyone would pay to see it." He smiled as he turned the page from the tree. "Check out the rap sheets on some of these guys."

Six pages were then turned over one by one, each with a different face and fact sheet to go along with it.

"Since those are from your files, I'm guessing they tie back to Tessa's case," she reasoned.

"You would be correct," he said. "I'm always going to be on the lookout for these men. One of whom is supposedly associated with the gunrunners."

"Houston, huh?" She shot him a look.

"We have a problem," he said.

"Okay, you already know I'm on board. There's one rule. No corny NASA jokes," she said.

"Does that mean we don't have a problem?" He laughed at his own witticism. Before she could protest, he added, "I'm just kidding. No more space humor. Scout's honor." He did a thing with his hand that was most certainly not the right gesture.

"Somehow I doubt you've ever been a Boy Scout," she muttered under her breath.

QUINT HADN'T KNOWN what the outcome would be when he'd shown up at Ree's mother's ranch. One of the last things he expected was to be at her house, discussing the case. He'd shown up on a whim, one that was paying off.

"Thank you," he said in all sincerity.

"Don't thank me now," she stated with more than a hint of mischief in her eyes. "Save it for when we put these jerks behind bars."

"What about Preston?" He would be a jerk if he didn't help her see what she might be giving up for this life. "He seems like a nice guy, Ree."

Shock stamped her features.

"I caught you off guard. Sorry about that," he said.

"No. Don't be." She blinked a couple of times, like that might somehow help her switch topics.

"I wasn't trying to ambush you, Ree. I promise," he stated.

"Do you seriously want to talk to me about my relationship with Preston?" Her cheeks flamed, making her even more beautiful. And, no, he didn't want to discuss her ex-boyfriend, but she needed to.

"I've been around the block a few times while working this job," he began. "If you look at our fellow agents, the divorce rate gets pretty high."

"Meaning?" She studied him.

"This job isn't easy on spouses, let alone new relationships," he continued, treading lightly. "I do realize it isn't my place to tell you one way or the other how to handle your personal life."

"You're right about one thing," she stated. "Okay, maybe two. The divorce rate is high. This job isn't easy on new relationships. But Preston and I aren't exactly new to each other, and I'm not seeing him. He's my brother's best friend, and I'm pretty certain my mom is responsible for him showing up at Sunday barbecue. I can say with one hundred percent honesty that I had nothing to do with it. So why the lecture?"

"It's not. Take away what you will from this conversation. All I'm trying to tell you is that a good person is worth slowing down for. Because if you spend all your time invested in work, that's all you'll have at the end of the day." There. He'd said his piece. He would leave it at that.

"You sound like my mother," she said. The blow struck hard in the center of his chest.

"I believe in your work and think you're a damn fine agent," he said by way of defense.

"Good. Because marriage and family aren't everything they're cracked up to be, you know," she said. "Some people don't even want children."

"Seriously?" He couldn't hide the shock in his voice.

"Not you, too." She rolled her eyes and smacked her flat palm against the table.

"I already told you that I'm not some macho jerk who believes women should be chained to the kitchen," he said. "I just thought that since you came from a big family you might like to have the same thing for yourself one of these days."

"You were just at my mother's house, right?" Her voice sounded incredulous.

"Yes," he said.

"And you were witness to how frustrating a big family is," she stated. And then she seemed to catch herself, remembering that he'd had just the opposite growing up. "Right. Sorry. I know our upbringings were very different."

"When I first walked up, the place looked like a Norman Rockwell painting," he stated.

"You do realize that's the fantasy. The 'real' involves fighting and people constantly sticking their noses in your business," she stated.

"Having people who care whether or not you live

or die doesn't seem like such a hardship," he admitted. In truth, he didn't dwell on the past. There were few people he'd ever talked to about the school liaison officer Quint credited with saving his life. He'd told Ree the whole story, figuring they needed to know each other's backgrounds in order to sell the newlywed concept. And yet he'd been on similar assignments before without divulging so many details from his past. The only person who knew about his background was his best friend, Tessa Kind. And she was dead.

The tension in Ree's facial muscles softened.

"I'm sorry" was all she said. Those two words washed over him. Not because she said them but because of the compassion in her eyes and in her voice while she spoke.

"I know," he said, and meant it. There was something special about Ree that he didn't want to spend a whole lot of time analyzing. The few kisses they'd shared still haunted him as the best he'd ever experienced. Going there while on an assignment seemed like the quickest way to let everything get out of hand.

Besides, he'd gotten what he came for. She'd agreed to take the case. They would head out to Houston to continue the marriage cover story as he moved on a man named Constantin, who was another step closer to Dumitru. Quint's growing feelings for her would only help him stay sharp. And moving forward, he would need to be as much on his game as he ever had been.

"I better pack so we can get on the road," Ree said.

"Sounds like a plan," he stated. "I'll give Agent Grappell a call to get us set up for the night." Grappell was the desk agent assigned to the case. He worked with them on the Cricket Creek case as well, and would be an asset to the team in Houston.

Maybe with Ree on board he could finally find justice for Tessa.

Chapter Four

"We'll work the same cover as before," Quint said to Ree as she sat in the passenger seat with the opened file on her lap. "As a newly married couple who are very much in love."

"I'm guessing the boot comes back on, then," she said, studying the tree drawing.

"It's a good way to counter my size, but we can ditch it," he said. They needed to make him seem like less of a threat to lower a target's defenses. The trick had worked like magic in Cricket Creek, but it came with its downsides. For instance, him forgetting to put it on.

"So you'll have walked away from your moving business due to this injury that came from moving a piano," she said, reviewing the facts.

"That's right," he confirmed. "Just no boot this time. I'm healing."

"And we had our first date at the pizza place on Third Street in Austin," she continued.

"There's no better place for craft pizza," he said with a smile.

"And Ronnie always comes out to check on the table when you order the day's special," she said.

Quint nodded.

"You'll be restocking, washing glasses and keeping the bartender happy as a barback in a popular country-and-western bar this time, so no heavy trays of food to carry," he said.

"No heavy food trays to carry." She didn't mind that part so much.

"This place is supposedly frequented by guys who are associated with Dumitru. One of the girlfriends of someone high up in the operation is a bartender there. Her name is Lola, and her boyfriend's name is Constantin," Quint said. "Your job is to try to get as close to her as possible."

"Got it," she said.

"Word of warning, Constantin goes by the name Lights Out because he likes to kill people while they're sleeping." Quint's tone was all business now.

This definitely made her realize they'd moved up the crime scale a few notches. This case had the potential to be even riskier, the criminals more violent and dangerous. Then there was Quint's lack of objectivity to consider. She had to trust he would step back when necessary. And yet knowing him and how determined he was to get to Dumitru, that might be asking the impossible.

"Before we get into this, I need to know you'll listen to me if I say it's time to pull back," Ree said. He shot her a look that said he didn't appreciate the comment. She put her hands in the air in the surrender position. "I've gotten to know you pretty well recently, and I've noticed that once you get on a trail, you don't let up. The trait is great for a case when it's applied at the right time and for the right reasons."

"But?"

"I think we both know what comes next without me spelling it out," she said.

Anger radiated off him in palpable waves. To his credit, he gripped the steering wheel tighter and clamped his mouth shut. They both knew she was right. The fact that he didn't argue made her believe he might just listen to her in a sticky situation.

"Noted," he finally said. "And I give you my word."

His promise was good enough for her. Time would tell if he could stay true to his word. In the meantime, she wouldn't overthink it.

"I'm guessing since this is Houston that I'll be working a honky-tonk," she said.

"And you'd be wrong," he said with a smirk.

"What? No cowgirl boots this time?" She feigned disappointment.

"You get to wear tuxedo shorts, suspenders and a red bow tie," he said.

"Please tell me this is not a strip club," she begged.

"It's a trendy place," he said. "The barbacks have a different outfit than bartenders and waitresses. You'll have the most skin covered. But you'll have to wear black fishnet stockings every night so I'm not sure how you feel about that."

"Great," she said. "I'd rather have on those and be fully covered, thank you very much."

"You won't get an argument from me there," he said, surprising her with his honesty and protectiveness over her. It wasn't the same as she was used to from Preston and her mother. Theirs made her feel like she was incompetent at her job. Quint's concern for her came from a place of not wanting her to be forced into doing something she wasn't comfortable with, which wasn't the same thing. He believed in her and came across as proud of her for being capable in her profession. His protectiveness wasn't suffocating.

"Do you have a picture of Lola by chance?" Ree asked.

"It's grainy," he said, pulling into a downtown apartment building garage. "You'll be working at a bar in the GreenStreet area. This place is within walking distance. It's a studio, so tight quarters, but we don't have a whole lot of belongings, and it's fully furnished."

"Corporate apartments?" she asked, figuring the ones rented by companies for business travelers were normally the ones that came set up and ready to go.

"That's right," he said. "All we need to do is unpack our clothes. I'll set up my laptop at the bar-height counter separating the kitchen from the living space."

Ree nodded. They'd spent a week in a one-room cabin on their last case and did fine. This shouldn't present a problem.

"We're on the seventh floor this time," he said. "Agent Grappell said Lola lives in the same building on nine."

"Maybe we'll run into each other in the elevator," Ree said.

Ree glanced at the number on the wall where he'd parked. Their spot was number thirteen. She hoped it wasn't an ominous sign.

"What's our apartment number?" she asked.

"Seven-three it is," he said with a smile.

At least the two of them were off to a better start than on the last case, where she'd tried to lay down the law on day one and he'd planted a kiss that still made her lips sizzle every time she thought about it.

She grabbed her bag as he disappeared into a door marked Elevators. He returned with a cart that looked like something a bellman would bring. Folks must move in and out of the building frequently if these were at the ready. It made sense when she thought about the fact that several of these apartments were used as corporate housing. Businesspeople would show up with nothing more than a couple of suitcases and whatever technology allowed them to do their jobs.

Ree waited until the cart was loaded and they were safely in apartment 73 before asking the question that had been on her mind since they'd parked. "Does Lola live here with her boyfriend?"

"From what Agent Grappell could uncover, Lights Out visits her and spends a lot of time here, but he has a house in Galveston on the bay side. His brother lives with him, and Grappell didn't have a whole lot of intel on the brother," Quint stated.

"That sounds suspect," Ree said. The only people who avoided being in the system were criminals. Big-time drug dealers were known to "borrow" vehicles or hire drivers rather than own one so the registration couldn't be traced back to them. She always knew someone was a lifetime criminal when she went back to find their picture in a high school yearbook only to discover there was none. People who intended to live a life of crime from an early age went to extremes to ensure there was no trail that could easily identify them.

"My thoughts exactly," he agreed as he stood in the middle of the room. "Home sweet home."

"Home" was an open space with a kitchen that could best be described as a kitchenette. One person could fit inside there, and it would be a stretch for someone Quint's size. The entryway was barely big enough for him to turn around in without bumping into a wall, but the room opened up nicely and the back wall was basically all glass, allowing for a ton of light. Their last place, the cabin in tiny Cricket Creek, Texas, had been much darker.

"It's very modern and clean. I'll give it that," Ree said as she stepped into the middle of the living area. Around the corner from the kitchen was a raised platform and niche that held the bed. A wall of closets was to one side. "Is there laundry?"

"In the building, just not in the apartment," he said.

The furniture was sleek and modern with clean lines. It was basically what she expected from a downtown Houston apartment.

"This place looks like something out of a magazine," she said, walking over to the closet with her suitcase. "I can't say the furniture looks especially comfortable. It's not exactly what you'd be able to sink into to watch a movie, but it does look chic."

"My thoughts exactly," Quint said. "It's like living in a museum where you'd be afraid to mess anything up."

"Everything has its place," she agreed. "The bed is decent-sized, though. And it looks comfortable for a good night of sleep."

"I can take the couch," he said.

"Not again," she countered. "This bed is big enough for both of us. You can stay to your side. We can put a row of pillows in between us. But I won't let you sacrifice sleep again." She shot him a look. "No arguing."

"I wouldn't want to fight with my wife," Quint fired back with a smirk. "You know the old saying, *happy wife, happy life*."

Ree rolled her eyes.

"You know I can see you, right?" he said.

"That's the whole point," she said before unpacking her suitcase and offering to do the same for him.

"I got it," he said, moving next to her and taking over a third of the closet. He had a pretty basic wardrobe of jeans and black T-shirts.

"I don't know if you're trying to sell the whole 'tech worker' bit, but your wardrobe fits the lifestyle," Ree said when she examined his clothes. Quint had posed as a tech student on their last assignment as well. It was meant to be a second career after selling the moving business he'd started with a partner.

Quint laughed. "No one has ever complained about my clothing style before."

Tech workers were notorious for having a closet full of basically the same clothes—jeans and T-shirts. The idea being that the brain could only handle a certain number of decisions each day before paralysis set in. The Silicon Valley set didn't want to waste one of those on clothes. It was smart when Quint really thought about it and made him feel a whole lot less lazy about his wardrobe.

"I didn't say it looked bad on you," she said as her cheeks turned a couple shades of pink. Ree turned away from him and picked pretend lint from a dress hanging in the closet.

Rather than reply, he said, "We should probably get a feel for the building and grab supplies."

"When do I interview for the barback job?" she asked.

"Done deal. The agency has an in with the club owner. You start tomorrow, and your uniform will be ready when you check in for work. Randy Halo owns several bars. He married a supermodel a few years back. She got into some trouble. The agency got her out in exchange for information. To make a long story short, she still owes the agency, and her husband doesn't want a criminal element in his club. He runs legitimate businesses and wants to keep his licenses," Quint explained.

"Good for him," she said. "Plus, a bar owner keeping a liquor license seems pretty important to keep the doors open."

"Lucky for us, he saw it in the same way," Quint said.

"Or lucky for him. Otherwise, it doesn't sound like he'd have much of a business right now," she quipped.

"Very true," Quint agreed. "Sadly, you're going to have to stay on your feet for entire shifts again."

"Nothing a bucket of ice won't cure," she said. "Before we get too deep in the case, mind if I check on my grandfather? He was most likely running late earlier, but I'd feel better if I heard it from him. You know?"

"Knock yourself out," he said. "I'll be in the kitchen to give you some privacy."

They both laughed at his comment when they glanced around the room. The kitchen wouldn't provide much solitude, but the gesture counted for something.

Quint moved into the other room and checked the fridge. He could open the fridge and freezer without hitting anything, and he could turn around in the space. That was the extent of his ability to move. Ree was quiet in the next room, and he took it as a bad sign.

A minute later, she showed up at the counter between the kitchen and living space. She claimed a barstool and blew out a breath, setting her cell phone down in front of her.

"No answer." She motioned toward the time showing on her phone. "And it's barely eight o'clock."

"Did you leave a message?" Quint asked. He didn't hear her, but that wasn't proof. She could have spoken quietly into the phone.

She shook her head.

"I texted him instead," she said. "Our cell phones aren't compatible, so his doesn't always register when I call and vice versa."

"The last person I dated had a problem with our incompatible phones," he said. "I'm pretty certain it's the reason we broke up. She would call and I wouldn't get the notification. When I didn't return her call in a reasonable amount of time, she thought I was out playing the field."

"You wouldn't do that to someone you cared about," Ree said without hesitation.

"Tell that to Amber," he said.

"Amber's the one missing out, then," Ree said without stopping to think much about her words. How did she understand him better than someone he'd spent six months getting to know? Not that he was complaining. All good partnerships started with a fundamental knowledge of each other's personalities and ticks.

"I couldn't agree with you more," he said. "But she seems happier with Todd."

"What kind of name is Todd?" she said with a smirk.

"I know…right?" He kept the joke alive. They both knew there wasn't anything wrong with the name. It was common.

"Were you in love?" Ree asked without looking up from her screen.

"With Todd?" he balked.

Ree shot him a look that would make any high schooler sit up and take note.

"I cared about her," he said.

"Not the same thing, and we both know it," she countered.

"It's as close as I can get," he said in all honesty. Too bad his answer seemed to cause her to deflate.

A knock at the door caused them both to jump, and the tense moment happening between them passed.

Chapter Five

"Who is it?" Ree asked, checking through the peephole at her new apartment. Quint drew his weapon, flipped off the kitchen light and stood at the ready a few feet away from the door. Quint produced their wedding rings from his front pocket before handing one over.

"Angie," said a female voice. She sounded college age and not much more.

Ree opened the door.

"You just moved in, right?" Angie asked. She was five feet three inches of tiny frame and thick horse-mane blond hair.

Ree folded her arms, leaned against the doorjamb and smiled. "That's right. My husband and I are still unpacking."

It was a tiny lie.

Angie had a dotting of freckles across her nose and an enthusiastic disposition, like cheerleader perky. She was a cutie but couldn't be much more than twenty-two.

"I live next door with my boyfriend," Angie said. "We've been here for a few months but haven't really made any friends in the building yet. I've been studying for my LSAT while Brad works. My parents think my roommate is one of my best friends from college. They'd kill me if they knew I was living with Brad."

"Where does Brad work?" Ree asked, figuring it never hurt to get the lay of the land since there was a total of four apartments on this floor. Angie must have been watching them through her peephole. They'd been careful not to say anything that could blow their cover in the garage or on the way inside the apartment.

"He's a fireman." Angie's eyes lit up at every mention of her boyfriend.

"Cool job," Ree said for lack of anything better. She'd been told she could get away with saying she was still in her late twenties, so she let her shoulders round a bit and put on a bigger smile.

"Right?" Angie said. She looked Ree up and down. "Do you work out?"

"When I can," Ree admitted.

"The building has a great gym on the second floor. They bring in CrossFit classes and Zumba," Angie said. "You do Zumba, right?"

"Yes. CrossFit is a little too intense for me," Ree said, twirling a lock of hair with her index finger as she tilted her head to one side.

"Same here, but Brad is obsessed." Angie's eyes lit up again. She seemed like a sweetheart. "But he also likes weights. He says CrossFit is bad for building muscles."

"I'm more of a runner," Ree said. "If I take a class, it would probably be Pilates."

"I love Pilates." Angie clasped her hands together and bounced.

"Maybe we'll take class together sometimes," Ree said before adding, "I should get back to unpacking. I start my job tomorrow, and we have so much to do. The fridge is empty, and we haven't had dinner yet."

"Okay. It was really nice meeting you," Angie said before leaning back on the heels of her tennis shoes. She waved as she took a step back.

"Same to you. And I'm serious about Pilates," Ree said as she slowly closed the door, watching which apartment Angie headed toward. Apartment 2. Ree made a mental note that Angie and Brad lived in 72 as she closed and then locked the door.

"Looks like you made a friend," Quint said, flipping on the light before returning his weapon to his ankle holster.

"Since Lola lives in the building and she's twenty-five, I might run into her at the gym. She might take classes, and now I'll have a buddy to introduce me around. I get the impression Angie is social. She's the type who would chat up a stranger at the gym," Ree said.

Quint nodded. "I got the same impression."

"Are you hungry?" she asked.

"Starving," he confirmed.

"Me, too. Shall we go grab dinner out?"

Quint nodded, then gave Ree a once-over. "We should grab a drink while we're out."

Ree knew exactly what he had in mind.

"It wouldn't hurt to figure out what my new place

of employment looks like," she said with a smile. Then she glanced down at what she had on. "Just give me a few minutes to change clothes and freshen up, and I'll be ready."

"You look perfect in my book," Quint said so low she almost didn't hear him. He crossed the room to the cabinet wall and grabbed a fresh pair of jeans and one of the few collared shirts he'd brought. It was black as pitch, and her heart skipped a few beats thinking how damn good he was going to look in it.

Fifteen minutes later, they looked like a very different couple as they exited the apartment and then the building. Despite the downtown area having plenty of lights, there were shadows cast everywhere. So many places to hide in plain sight, Ree thought as the prickly feeling of being watched crept over her.

She reached for Quint's hand and then leaned into him as she surveyed the area, pretending to take in the restaurants and bars.

"How about tacos?" Quint asked, squeezing her hand. The move shouldn't be as reassuring as it was. He realized what she was doing, and this was his way of acknowledging it. He lifted their clasped hands and pressed a tender kiss to the back of hers. The move sent a sensual shiver skittering up her arm.

The watched feeling returned.

"That's not a fair question. Always tacos," she teased, trying to force lightness she didn't feel.

Quint guided them across the street to a corner restaurant. The place was small and crowded. They got in line just inside the door to place their orders when

Quint tugged her toward him and wrapped his arms around her. She turned her face to the side, to the glass door and wall of windows, and scanned the area to see if anyone had followed them. It shouldn't come as a surprise that no one seemed to have, except for the eyes-on-her feeling she'd had on the way over.

The line moved inch by inch.

"All I can say is these better be the best tacos I've ever had in my life," she warned as her stomach growled.

Quint dipped his head and pressed a kiss to her lips, and she got lost in his masculine scent for just a few seconds as she looked into those sapphire-blue eyes of his. Eyes like those should be outlawed. She could stare into them all day. *And night*, a wicked little voice in the back of her mind added. The voice was up to no good, and that was exactly what would come of her falling for this agent…no good.

Still, standing here, she couldn't help but be under his spell while his arms looped around her waist, holding her so close she could feel his heartbeat as it raced against his ribs. A little piece of her hoped she was having the same effect on him as he had on her.

Both seemed to realize touching that hot stove would set the whole house ablaze. For one moment, Ree couldn't help but think how incredible it would be to dance in the flames if only for a little while.

And then she recognized a face from Quint's file. The midtwenties male stepped inside the restaurant and moved behind a group of three people so they blocked Ree's view of him. It dawned on her that Quint had been on the bust that had killed his partner, Tessa Kind, and the two of them were currently chasing the same group down. What if Quint was recognized?

QUINT FELT THE exact moment every single one of Ree's muscles tensed up. Her body, flush with his, gave her away. She looked up at him with those emerald green eyes that made him lose his train of thought, and then subtly nodded her head toward the door.

He shifted to the left as they took another step closer to the order counter. Music thumped, giving the feeling they were already in a nightclub. This place must make amazing tacos to have a constant line at nine thirty on a Sunday night.

Ree moved to the beat. With her body against his, concentrating on anything else took effort. He took another step backward at her urging. They were getting close enough for him to turn around and check out the menu that was above the pair of order takers. As he turned, the profile of a male from the past came into view.

Quint pressed his hand against Ree's back, tapping his fingers and giving a slight nod as he turned, turning his back to the male. Quint couldn't put a name to the familiar face. It had to be in his files back at the apartment, locked in the tackle box that was still in the back seat of the truck that had been assigned to the case.

This was going to bother him until he got back to the files. Was Mystery Guy associated with Constantin? Could Quint somehow get a picture to jar his memory later? As it was, the guy's profile was familiar, but Quint could be reaching. Ree had locked onto the Mystery Guy first. Had he followed them into the taco joint? Did he recognize Quint from the bust?

Ree cleared her throat and pressed a hand to Quint's chest.

"Honey," she said, urging him to move another step toward the order counter. They'd decided on their last assignment that "honey" was acceptable but "babe" was fingernails on a chalkboard to them both. They'd detailed out the rules of engagement. They'd shared information about each other, like the fact that her favorite color was blue and her second-favorite color was green. They'd decided to call each other by their rightful first names in public and he'd had documents made up with the last name Matthews. He just realized he'd forgotten to give her wallet to her. His had the credit cards and his driver's license, but hers was a different story.

Quint's turn to order would be next, so he spent a minute studying the menu before deciding on two number threes. Ree went with two brisket tacos. They ordered a pair of beers before being handed a buzzer and told to step aside. This whole scenario was a lot like ordering at Starbucks, minus the pager. He didn't take it as a good sign they needed one in the first place.

Taking the couple of steps, he glanced over his shoulder. He located the trio but not Mystery Guy. Quint's gaze flew to the glass door as it was closing behind a male figure leaving the line.

He bit back a curse and the urge to follow. Instead, he tugged his "wife" against him, her back to his chest, and whispered, "He's leaving."

She reached for his hand and then squeezed. The implication that this guy got what he wanted—confirmation he'd found Quint—loomed in the air.

The pager went off. They made their way to the pickup counter. Ree took the pager and then set it in the basket with others as a smiling kid who couldn't be a day over eighteen handed them a tray.

Ree thanked him as Quint grabbed their dinner tray, then followed her to a table outside and on the side of the restaurant in a space sectioned off for restaurant guests. It was warm out but not unbearably hot for a change. Quint set the tray down. Ree pulled their taco baskets off the tray and set them up with their beers before Quint took the tray to its return spot on top of the garbage can next to the exit. He used this as an opportunity to skim the area for Mystery Guy.

He was nowhere in sight.

"Damn," Quint said, returning to the table.

Ree gave a slight nod before picking up a taco. She cleared her basket in a matter of minutes and stopped talking in the process.

"You really must have been starving," he said to her.

"I wasn't kidding earlier." She wiggled her eyebrows at him as she wiped her mouth clean. He probably shouldn't let his gaze linger on those kissable lips of hers. Frustration at the missed opportunity to get a good look at Mystery Guy had Quint tied up in knots.

If his cover was blown on the first day, he couldn't let Ree walk into that bar alone tomorrow night. Mystery Guy had no doubt seen the two of them together.

If this guy was related to the case, life just got a whole lot messier for Quint and Ree.

"I feel like I might have seen Mystery Guy before in your files," Ree said.

"We can check when we get home," Quint offered.

Ree nodded.

"Ready?" he asked as she finished the last sip of her beer.

"Sure am," she said, pushing up to standing and gathering her trash. Disposal was easy. Their table was taken almost immediately.

"Did you like your dinner?" she asked, leaning into him as he put an arm around her shoulder.

"No taco has the right to taste as good as those," he quipped with a forced smile, in an attempt to lighten the mood.

Ree laughed, and the sound was almost musical.

Quint needed to shake off the gloom-and-doom feeling before it took hold. A strong mindset was the most important asset he could bring to an undercover operation. Mystery Guy might have been a random person who'd decided against waiting too long for tacos no matter how good they were. It wasn't a crime to leave a line he'd barely been in. If the same guy turned up at the bar, Quint would grab Ree and explain the situation. As it was, checking him against the photos in the file could wait.

Besides, she'd already picked up on the guy and would be watching out for him. She'd realized something could have been up with the man.

The Houstonian NightClub, HNC, was a five-minute

walk from the taco restaurant, so roughly eight minutes from home. Driving Ree to and from work would leave them less exposed, but it was too close and would cast suspicion if anyone was paying attention.

Music could be heard thumping from halfway down the block. HNC took up two levels. A staircase to the left and above the bar was made of some kind of material that looked a lot like glass. A couple of guys sat strategically at the bar below, occasionally glancing up to check out the ladies in short skirts who were on the stairs. Sexist jerks.

Quint was more than a little relieved for Ree that she wouldn't be subjected to another uniform like the one at Greenlight on their last case. He did note, however, that the waitresses were attractive. The bartenders were drop-dead gorgeous and seemed to be the attraction. There was a mix of men and women behind the bar, mostly the latter. Waitresses wore less clothing than barbacks. They had on the same tuxedo shorts, but theirs fell higher on their legs, and the unbuttoned tuxedo shirt barely covered their breasts. There must have been a workout requirement to be a waitress, because they all had abs most would kill for. They also had tiny waists and larger-than-normal breasts. Some were blondes and others varying shades of brown, but HNC definitely had a type for their personnel.

A bar covered an entire wall to the left. There were tables and sofas almost like he'd seen in five-star hotels. To the right was a dance floor with an extensive lighting system that would rival any concert he'd ever been to. Guys were dressed in every variety of black shirt possible, and the women were glammed up, full makeup and hair, and looking like they'd just walked off a runway or red carpet. The median age for the women was thirty. Meanwhile, the men averaged higher. There was a mix of distinguished gray-haired men with women who looked like supermodels on their arms and youngish, newer-money men. New money always wore the most bling. The best way to tell how much money an older guy had was by how expensive his watch was. This place could be a showroom for Rolex. The women looked like they were in one of those reality shows about who could marry a millionaire.

And at the far end of the bar...Mystery Guy.

Chapter Six

Ree must've seen Mystery Guy from the taco stand at the same time as Quint, based on how much his muscles involuntarily tensed. She navigated them to an open table on the opposite side of the bar before scanning for Lola. As it turned out, all Ree had to do was follow Mystery Guy's lead. He was ordering a drink from someone who matched Lola's description.

In fact, there was a run on drinks at Lola's end of the bar, considering the number of single men who seemed uninterested in any of the women in the area. This area of the bar was lit in sea-blue lighting, which made it a little easier to see. Lola had black hair that ran halfway down her back. Even from Ree's position across the room, it was easy to see Lola was beautiful. She had a look that was difficult to pinpoint. European? Latin American?

This whole situation would be so much easier if Ree could just walk into the bar, flash a badge and start interviewing people. Of course, she also knew that would be the death of a sting operation. These cases took a whole lot more finesse. Was that part of the thrill?

Constantin was nowhere to be found. Apparently, Mystery Guy wasn't ordering a drink, because he nodded at Lola, smiled and then headed toward the door. Was he leaving?

The move caught Ree off guard and she didn't want to be seen by him twice in one night, so she immediately hopped on Quint's lap and wrapped her arms around him, shielding much of her face. To hide the rest, she whispered, "Sorry." And then she planted a kiss on Quint's lips that sent her own pulse racing.

He deepened the kiss, causing her stomach to free-fall. This didn't seem like the time to compare this kiss to their last back in Cricket Creek, but this one easily blew the other one away. And that was saying something. There was a hunger and urgency in their movements as their tongues collided, searching and teasing. Beer had never tasted so good on someone else's lips before.

Had it really been less than a week since their case ended? Because this felt like a lovers' reunion kiss after being separated for months.

Ree forced herself not to read too much into it as she pulled away enough to ensure Mystery Guy was walking out the door. He was, and he never looked back. Ree exhaled, trying to slow her erratic heartbeat. She couldn't help but smile as she leaned in to his ear and whispered, "He's gone."

Quint brought his hands around to cup her face before laying a tender kiss on her lips. Then he pulled back and pressed his forehead against hers. "What are you drinking?"

"Whatever the most popular drink is," she said, figuring there was some type of signature cocktail at a place like this. There weren't a whole lot of beers in hand when she'd scanned the room after walking in. This was a mixed-drink crowd.

He hesitated with her still on his lap, so she scooted off and claimed the other chair at the table. He shook his head, and she was almost certain she heard him say the word *damn*.

Having an effect on the legendary Agent Quinton Casey probably shouldn't be such a source of pride. Except there was something about this man that rattled her to the core. This wasn't the time or the place to dig into finding out what that was. While he moved to the bar, she checked her phone. Still no word from her grandfather.

Everything had to be okay, though. Her family knew better than to interrupt her while she was in deep undercover. If anything had happened to her grandfather, someone would have reached out to her by now. He'd most likely just let his phone run out of battery and forgot to charge it. He wasn't nearly as tied to his cell as Ree was. The thought of being without hers caused her chest to squeeze with anxiety. Had she become too dependent on it? Probably.

And yet it proved useful time and time again on investigations. She needed to grab her assigned cell phone and lock her personal one in the tackle box. Could she touch base with home one more time before she did?

During her last assignment, she'd kept her personal cell phone on her. It had been a mistake when Shane had called and upset her. Since the risks on this case went up considerably, she wouldn't take any chances her personal information or contacts could be jeopardized no matter how much she wanted an update on her grandfather.

Ree tucked her cell back inside her handbag as Quint made his way over with cocktails in hand. His came in a highball glass whereas hers looked like a beach-blue martini. It required skill to make it through the crowd, which was thickening by the second, without spilling.

He set both drinks on the wooden tabletop with a grin as a few heads turned after he'd walked past. Jealousy wasn't something Ree normally could be accused of. Quint brought out a different side to her. She chalked it up to being protective over her new partner who was supposed to be her husband.

"You have many talents I had no idea about," Ree said as he reclaimed his seat opposite her.

"The drinks cost almost as much as my first car," he said with a laugh. Despite the jokes he'd been making tonight, the concern lines etching his forehead told a different story. He was worried about this one no matter how much he tried to hide it. She doubted anyone else could tell, but she'd gotten very good at reading him on the last case.

"Our building isn't cheap," she said, referring to the fact that Lola lived on the ninth floor. Ree had automatically assumed Constantin paid for the apartment, and that might very well be true, but Lola might be able to finance the place on her own with the kinds of tips she should be making in a place like this.

"That it is not," Quint said, holding out his arm. "I need a new watch."

"You have the exact kind of watch a student should wear," she said. On their last assignment, his cover was that he left the moving business he owned to go to school for a day job working on computers. "Besides, we'll be living off a percentage of the tips bartenders make for at least the next year while you finish your certification."

"Maybe I should stay with what I know," he quipped.

"We talked about this, honey," she said, putting on a show of frustration in case anyone was paying attention.

Glancing over at Lola, Ree wondered if she could pop over and introduce herself. Tell the bartender that Ree was a new hire and would start work tomorrow. Lola seemed to be the busiest bartender in the whole place.

After a few minutes passed, she thought better of interrupting Lola while she seemed to be jamming.

"You're right. Stick to the plan," he conceded. "By the time this ankle fully heals, I'll be working a corporate nine-to-five."

"That's the idea," she said. "And I'll be a 'kept' woman." She made air quotes over the word *kept*. It was good practice for them to get into character in a loud bar where music thumped. It would also make listening in on Lola's conversations trickier, Ree figured.

"Let me know whenever you're ready to go finish unpacking," Quint said before downing his drink.

She'd been sipping on hers. A quick glance around,

and the rubber plant next to her got a splash of vodka and whatever made the drink blue. It tasted good, but she wasn't a big drinker and could still feel the beer from dinner.

She made a show of setting her glass down on the wooden tabletop. "I'm ready whenever you are."

Quint stood up at the same time she did, putting them toe-to-toe. She glanced up at him, locking eyes, in a near-fatal mistake when they stood this close. He cracked a smile that was worth more than a thousand words, dipped his head and kissed her. This time, he didn't deepen the kiss.

He very well could have for the effect it had on her.

"Nice" was all she said as she took a step back, thinking she didn't need to get too used to this. Because she could really go there with a person like Quint.

QUINT REACHED FOR Ree's hand and then linked their fingers. The pace of the eight-minute walk home was a fast one. He scanned both sides of the street, searching for Mystery Guy. There was no sign of him on either sidewalk. The thought that he could live in one of the buildings around here disturbed Quint. The guy could be watching them right now. He instinctively tugged Ree a little closer at the thought. He could protect her better if she was right next to him.

"I need to grab the tackle box out of the truck before we head up," Quint whispered to Ree.

She nodded, looking a little defeated. Her new cell phone would be inside, and she would have to hand her personal phone in.

"You haven't heard anything about your grandfather yet," he said.

"No, I haven't," she confirmed.

"I'm sorry, Ree. I know how important he is to you," Quint said, giving her hand a squeeze.

"I have to believe he's fine," she said. "And he probably is. If something had happened, my family would have contacted me by now, so I'm taking it as a positive sign they haven't."

"That's a good attitude as long as it feels right to take that approach," he said.

"It does," she stated with a little less enthusiasm. She was struggling, and there wasn't anything he could do about it. Unless…

"I could call your brother for you," he said. "Shane would recognize the number of my burner phone. I'd have a good chance he would pick up."

"No, but thank you," she said. "It's a sweet offer. Maybe I could send a text to apologize after blowing out of there. Let them know I'll be over after the case wraps to say I'm sorry in person."

"I'm sure they would appreciate the gesture," he said. "And in case you're worried about me calling him again, I deleted his number and all traces of it have been erased from the phone." Shane had given Ree bad advice on day one of the last operation and had convinced the agency to give him Quint's number. The move had caught Ree off guard, and Quint vowed never to go behind her back again when it came to her family. He should have told her right away when it happened but didn't, thinking he was protecting her relationship with her brother. It had had the opposite effect.

"I appreciate it, Quint," she said, taking the phone he held out to her. She sent the text, and a response came back almost immediately.

"Shane said he was very happy to hear from me," she stated with a broad smile.

They detoured to the garage, where he picked up the tackle box and a blanket she'd forgotten earlier. There was a throw pillow underneath that she grabbed to take upstairs and personalize the apartment a little, or so she'd said when she'd thrown it in the back seat.

Once back in the apartment, he spread photos out across the counter, searching for the familiar face from earlier.

"Do you see him?" Quint asked. All he knew was that Mystery Guy's hair was black and long enough to curl up at the collar. Quint wished he'd seen more than a flash of the guy. Flipping through the small stack of pictures, Quint couldn't find anyone with this guy's profile.

"Not yet," she said.

He sat on the stool and thumbed through the photos again, slowly this time. Shook his head when she didn't pinpoint anyone. "I could have sworn I recognized him from your file," she said.

"Maybe you got your wires crossed," he said. It happened. For now, Mystery Guy was just that…a mystery.

"It's late, and it's been a long day," Ree said with a small nod and smile. "I should probably get ready for bed."

She turned toward the bathroom, took a few steps, then paused at the doorway. "It means a lot coming from you, by the way."

"Anytime," he said. "And I mean it."

Quint thumbed through the photos once more, studying each even more carefully. Something niggled at the back of his mind, but he couldn't place it, and putting too much emphasis on it wouldn't help. He tucked the photos inside the folder before replacing them inside the tackle box. There wasn't much more that could be done until morning, so he locked the box, then put it inside the coat closet to the right of the door, figuring most wives wouldn't want a tackle box in the same cabinet where they kept their clothing.

Clearly, this one hadn't seen a boat, dock or fishing hole, but anyone who busted into the apartment wouldn't know that. Maintaining an image was important. Doing what was expected was necessary. If anything stood out as unusual, their cover would be in jeopardy.

Quint started making a mental checklist of everything that needed to be done in the morning. Groceries. Supplies, like a laundry basket and detergent. He could gather everything easily enough.

Ree emerged from the bathroom wearing a pair of cotton pajamas that hugged her curves a little too well. Quint cleared his throat.

"You're up in the bathroom," Ree said, her voice a little too sexy.

"Yep," he stated. "Your new cell phone is on the counter. I'll be out in a few minutes."

She walked over to the flyer on the counter.

"Pilates at nine o'clock tomorrow morning. I have a feeling my new buddy, Angie, will be there," she said.

"I'll hit the weights while you take the class," he said.

Angie seemed like the nosy-neighbor type. Could they get information from her about the building's other residents—residents like Lola?

Chapter Seven

Ree stretched her arms as she opened her eyes to the sunlight filling the apartment. The clock on the night-stand said it was already eight o'clock. Pilates was in an hour, which gave her time to grab coffee… Hold on. There was no coffee in the place. The kitchen was empty, and they hadn't gone out for supplies last night.

There was also no one sleeping beside her. Quint had been an early riser in the cabin, too. She'd conked out before he'd made it out of the bathroom last night. Did the man ever sleep? She hadn't heard him leave, either. But then, she'd always been a heavy sleeper. Came with being a Sheppard, if she could believe her older brother Shane. But then, he'd also said he hadn't slept since his three-year-old son had been born. With a new baby in the house, she wasn't sure how he did it.

Throwing the covers off, Ree slipped out of the comfortable bed in the quiet nook of the apartment. It only took a few steps for the rest of the apartment to be in full view, which she saw as a good sign.

Quint was hunkered over his laptop at the breakfast counter. He glanced over at her. "Good morning."

"It would be a better morning if I'd stopped off at the store for coffee grinds last night," she said, half teasing as she made her way to the bathroom. After freshening up and changing into yoga pants and a sports bra with a loose shirt over it, she stepped out almost ready to face the world.

Quint held up a mug.

"What is that?" she asked.

"Maybe you should check for yourself," he said with a smirk.

Ree wasted no time racing over to him. "Coffee? How?"

"I got up early and didn't want to disturb you, so I ran to the store," he said before going back to studying his laptop like he wasn't a hero. "Made a pot and figured you would want a cup when you got up."

"You are seriously amazing. You know that, right?" she said.

"If you think that's impressive, I stopped off for bagels, too." He wiggled his eyebrows at her, which made her laugh. This man was one of the best agents she would ever hope to work with, and he had serious food skills. He'd kept her caffeinated and well fed on the last undercover operation, and here he was doing it again.

She moved around to the other side of the counter. The bag was sitting next to a stainless-steel toaster. What the place lacked in space, it made up for in style. All the appliances were top-of-the-line. In some ways, this kitchen was perfect, because she could literally reach every cabinet in any direction by taking a step to her left or to her right. She would never be accused of being chef material, but if she had to cook, this kitchen would make it easy.

"I never want to have to work with another partner again," she said as she popped a bagel in the toaster. "Did you eat?"

"All done here," he said.

"What time did you get up?" She glanced at the sink and saw no dirty dishes.

"Five…give or take," he admitted, taking a sip of coffee. "I couldn't sleep."

"Was it because of Mystery Guy?" she asked, blowing on her fresh brew before taking a sip, and enjoying the burn on her throat.

"Partially," he admitted. "I'm also trying to figure out how to get myself a job where I can be close to you at the bar."

"I highly doubt we'll get lucky enough for you to get access to the computers like in the last case, despite our cover," she said.

"I had the same thought. Except most people aren't great with computers, so maybe we can find an in for me with someone at the bar," he said. "There has to be a way."

"If anyone mentions needing help, you know I'll mention you," she said. "I have a feeling that I'm going to be busy all night, though. Did you see how hopping the place was on a Sunday night?"

He nodded.

"Imagine what the weekends must be like," she said.

"You're starting on a Monday. Maybe that will give you a chance to get your bearings," he pointed out.

"What about Randy? Does he have cameras in the place?" she asked.

"He only places them in the back office," Quint stated.

"Can't he give you a job?" she asked.

"It'll be suspicious if a husband-and-wife team show up and suddenly both work for him," Quint said.

"That's a good point," she admitted. "Plus, it isn't like he's involved. He's fully cooperating."

Quint nodded.

Ree scarfed down the bagel almost the minute it popped up. The warm bread was exactly what she needed to power through a Pilates class with Angie. She polished off her coffee and rinsed out the mug. "Do you think I need to take my own towel?"

"They have some down at the gym," he informed. "I already checked it out for you."

"Nice. Thank you," she said, then realized she didn't have a yoga mat. "Do they, by chance, have mats downstairs?"

"Yours is rolled up by the door," he said. "I thought you might need one, so I picked one up while I was out. It's amazing what you can buy at the corner store in downtown Houston when you're out at a ridiculous time of the morning."

She laughed.

"I owe you one," she said. "Make that two considering you bought bagels and three when you consider the coffee… Hold on a minute. Are you trying to butter me up?" She folded her arms across her chest in a playful move. The case was dangerous and she took her work seriously, but these moments of brevity broke up the tension and allowed for breathing room, which was much needed considering cases extended days and sometimes weeks.

"Consider it a thank-you for taking the case," he said. The look he gave her said he meant it, too. "I wouldn't want anyone else having my back right now."

"You're welcome," she said, thinking how nice it was to work together. Could they be partners? Or would his past always keep him at arm's length?

Her answer came a few seconds later when she felt a wall come up between them. He shifted in his seat and redirected his focus to his laptop, and there was nothing she could do to bring him back. He'd experienced a level of hell she could only imagine in blaming himself for the death of his pregnant partner and best friend. Quint had been set to become the baby's godfather.

Quint had let his partner talk him into holding off on telling their boss about the pregnancy. Apparently, she'd asked for time so she could deliver the news on her own terms. The baby's father exited the picture after learning about the kid on the way. Then, during a bust with multiple agencies involved, Tessa was killed by friendly fire. Quint couldn't stop beating himself up. It was clear that he blamed himself, because he'd said Tessa and her baby would be alive right now if he'd stood his ground. Department policy would have had Tessa assigned to desk duty, and Quint would have gone into the bust alone. That was all true. But the part he was missing was that he couldn't accept the reality that he wasn't responsible for other people's choices. Lack of communication between agencies was responsible for Tessa's death. It was a harsh reality and serious risk when working with other agencies. Mistakes happened when busts were rushed.

Ree glanced at the time. Eight forty-five. Time to head downstairs to Pilates with Angie.

"I'm going down," she said to Quint. "Are you coming?"

"I'll be there in a bit," he said without looking up from his screen.

Ree grabbed the yoga mat and her key before heading downstairs. She figured getting there early would give her a chance to socialize with others in the building. She pressed the elevator button and waited. It came up quickly and by the time the ding sounded, a door opened behind Ree.

"Hey." Angie's perky voice shouldn't have surprised Ree.

She turned and greeted her neighbor.

"Looks like you're heading to class," Angie said, holding up her mat. "Same."

Angie stepped inside the elevator behind Ree and pulled the rubber band from her wrist before using it to tie her hair back. Had she heard Ree's door close? Had she been listening for it? Angie was either that nosy or that lonely. Firefighter hours could be to blame, considering they worked several days on and a couple of days off. It was probably great for studying but also most likely made for many dinners for one.

The good news was that Angie could end up being

a useful source of information. She seemed about as pure as the driven snow, so Ree didn't worry about Angie being involved in criminal activity. She might, however, have the scoop on the building.

"How's studying going?" Ree asked.

Angie exhaled in dramatic fashion. "Hard. It's hard. I took a practice test last night and got nowhere near the score I need."

"That's tough, but at least you have a baseline. Did you at least figure out what you needed to focus on?" Ree asked.

"I did, but this is going to be harder than I thought," Angie said. She held up her yoga mat. "I've taken enough of these classes to become a certified teacher." She laughed. "If the whole 'law school' thing doesn't work out I could have a real career doing this."

Angie rolled her eyes and Ree laughed. She was going to like taking class together.

The elevator dinged and the doors opened to the second floor.

"Wow." Ree glanced around, taking in the massive glass-enclosed space. "Does the gym take up the whole floor?"

"Yes. It's great, isn't it?" Angie said.

"I'm impressed." Ree walked the circle around the elevator bank, noticing a certain black-haired bartender stretching in one corner.

"Follow me," Angie said. "We're early. I'll take you on the tour."

"You know, I'm feeling a little stiff after sitting in a

truck yesterday during the move. Mind if we tour after class?" Ree asked. "I should probably stretch now."

QUINT PULLED OUT the tackle box and checked the photos again. There was still no sign of Mystery Guy. Whatever niggled at the back of Quint's mind frustrated him to no end, since the information was so close but just out of reach. Was it a piece of valuable intel? Was it unrelated and something from a past bust? Was it something that could mean the difference between life and death in this case?

He wasn't so worried about himself, but Ree's safety came to mind. What if Quint had knowledge that could end up getting her shot but couldn't access it until it was too late?

After logging in to the agency database, Quint had spent the morning checking through his old case files and came up short. His mind had always been sharp and his memory had been good as gold. The only explanation for the lapse was stress. So he needed to calm the hell down and get a grip or risk putting them both in more danger. Since that was unacceptable, he opened files from two years ago.

Forty-five minutes later, he realized he was going to miss his workout window if he didn't get changed and downstairs in five minutes. Ree had left the apartment early, but her class was in full swing by now. He'd heard the neighbor's door close and voices in the hallway. Angie must have been listening for Ree this morning. The woman was persistent. He would give her that much. Or bored. The second was likely considering the fact that her live-in boyfriend was a firefighter. Their schedules were demanding.

Quint figured Ree already realized how much of an asset Angie could be in learning who was who in the building. A smart, bored young person was a good bridge to the goings-on in the building but, damn, Quint was beginning to feel old. His body definitely screamed at him for being over forty and trying to keep the same muscle-punishing workouts. What could he say? It was hard to dial it down when he was used to breaking a good sweat and lifting a certain number when it came to weights.

He changed into something more suitable for the gym, figuring he could get away with an arms-only workout this morning. The injured ankle excuse would keep him from running in public, which had always been his go-to when he needed to clear his mind for a case. Then there was Tessa. His thoughts could go down a dark path there, especially when images of Tessa in his arms, taking her last breaths, assaulted him. She'd said she was sorry, but he didn't deserve the apology. In fact, it should have been the reverse. Tessa would be alive today if not for him.

Those thoughts got him moving toward the elevator to check on Ree. She was fully capable of doing her job, an equal in every way that counted. And yet he had to confirm she was okay with his own eyes.

The elevator doors opened almost immediately after he pushed the button. Had someone come to the floor while he was getting dressed? No doors had closed to his knowledge. He noted that he had to be close to the kitchen to hear activity in the hallway.

The ride down stopped at almost every floor and the elevator was jammed full by the time he reached number two.

"Excuse me," he said, navigating his way as people stepped aside and out to allow him to exit. He thanked them before surveying the area. The glass walls and doors made seeing into the gym easy enough.

He took a few steps and froze. Ree was on what looked like a midclass water break standing to the side of the room with Angie and Lola. Lola made eye contact and he did his best to hide his momentary shock. Did she catch him?

Chapter Eight

Ree saw Quint almost the second he entered the second floor. There was just something about his physical presence that made people stop and stare, herself included.

"Looks like your husband made it after all," Angie said.

"He's a keeper," Lola said, making eyes at Ree. "And he looks as good in workout clothes as he does in jeans."

"He sure is and he certainly does," Ree said. She didn't have to fake her appreciation for Quint's good looks. What could she say? The man was easy on the eyes.

"What happened to his foot, if you don't mind my asking?" Angie said.

"He owned a moving business and dropped a piano on his ankle," Ree said as the others winced. "It hurt like hell, but I think it's going to be good for us. Now he's working on certification in computer science and starting a new chapter in life."

"You must be set with insurance," Lola said, and Ree was beginning to see a practical nature come out.

"His business partner let insurance lapse without saying a word," Ree said. "We sold our half of the business, which sets us up for a few months and helps with medical bills, but that's why I'll be working at HNC."

"You should have stopped by and said hello last night," Lola stated.

"You seemed busy, and I figured we would meet tonight during my shift anyway," Ree said.

Lola smiled. It was a shame she was linked with Constantin.

"It'll be nice to know someone at work. We moved here for a fresh start," Ree said, playing the "new kid in town" card to her advantage.

"Of course. I remember when Esteban and I came to the States two years ago from Argentina. We didn't know anyone at first. But then I got the job at the bar and he found work. Life got better," Lola said.

"Is Esteban your husband?" Angie asked as her gaze dropped to Lola's ring finger. Having Angie around was so helpful. It kept Ree from having to ask a lot of intrusive questions. Leave it to a bored person who happened to be a social butterfly to do the work of ten investigators.

"No. No. Nothing like that." Lola shook her head for emphasis. "Esteban is my brother."

"Ohhhhh," Angie said. "That's really brave to leave your country and start over."

"I wasn't here long before I met my boyfriend, so it turned out fine." Lola's gaze dropped, and Ree saw there was a story there.

"It's good. It all worked out," Lola said, but there

was a wistful quality to her voice that Ree didn't need to be good at her job to pick up on.

Rather than let Angie continue digging, Ree decided to rescue the conversation. "The bar looked pretty busy last night. Is it always that crowded on a Sunday?"

Lola shot a thankful look at Ree, and she realized she'd just won major points.

"It is. The money is so good on the weekends," Lola said. "When do you start?"

"Tonight," Ree said with a tentative smile.

"You'll do great," Lola reassured. "Mondays are the slowest, so that'll give you a chance to figure things out before the Thursday night crowd hits. Thursdays through Sundays are our busiest. Believe me, you'll need to be ready for those." Lola turned to Angie. "You should come by. Take a break from studying."

"Maybe I will." Angie perked up. "My boyfriend is working tonight, and I don't think I can look at another screen for at least two days."

Lola's forehead wrinkled as questions formed behind her eyes.

"Angie's boyfriend is a fireman. And she's studying for the LSAT."

Angie practically beamed. She was one of the purest souls Ree had ever encountered. Good for her. Working at the agency had tainted Ree more than she cared to admit. It became obvious when she met a sweet soul like Angie just how much Ree had moved away from being a doe-eyed kid herself. Seeing the worst in society did that to a person. Of course, locking up the bad guys went a long way toward restoring her faith in humanity. Focusing on the good guys out there made it all worth it.

"Did you say your husband knows what to do with computers?" Lola asked, a slightly desperate quality in her eyes.

"He's good with them," Ree said.

"Mine has been turning off for no reason," Lola said. "Esteban has no idea what to do to fix it. Any chance your husband would be willing to take a look?"

"No promises, but it can't hurt for him to try," Ree said, stunned it was so easy to get Quint an in so quickly. "We can ask him after class."

The instructor had taken her place at the front of the room and was slowly stretching on her mat while turning the music up. Clearly, a hint to set down water bottles and rejoin her.

"Will he still be here?" Lola asked, motioning toward Quint.

"He should be. He's been all about chest and arms since the accident that injured his ankle," Ree said. "Living with him wasn't easy while he was in recovery and couldn't work out."

"I can't imagine," Lola said, and her horrified expression made Ree smile.

"Sounds rough," Angie agreed as they each took their mats with her in between. Buddying up to Angie had paid off big-time.

The back half of the class almost kicked Ree's behind. She was a runner and had taken the occasional hot yoga class. Pilates with weights had been harder than she'd expected. Then again, she'd been out of a workout routine for a couple of months now aside from going for the occasional run.

The instructor ended class with an inspirational quote and a deep bow. Ree was in serious need of a shower. She grabbed a towel and met Angie and Lola at the "hydration station" wondering why they couldn't just call it what it was…a water fountain. Then again, she figured the building owners could charge more in rent if everything sounded fancier than it was.

"Let me know when you're ready to meet my husband," Ree said to Lola.

"I don't want to disturb his workout," Lola said with a little headshake.

"He won't mind," Ree said. "But you could always come over later and bring your laptop with you. We're in apartment seven-three."

"I'm on the ninth floor, same apartment number," Lola said. "If you don't mind. I'd love to come by before work."

"How's three o'clock sound?" Ree asked.

"Perfect to me," Lola responded. She was genuinely likable, so the thought that she lived a double life with a man who went by the name Lights Out was surprising. But then, Ree had seen just about everything in her line of work. Nothing should surprise her anymore.

"Do you guys want to head out for breakfast?" Angie asked.

Something behind Angie caught Lola's eye.

"Excuse me," she said.

Ree turned in time to see Mystery Guy from last

night standing at the gym's door. There was no way he was Constantin, so why was he here?

"How about you?" Angie asked, focusing on Ree.

"Sorry. I ate before I came down," she said. "I better let my husband know we're having company later. You're welcome to stop by if you'd like."

Ree had made the offer out of courtesy, not expecting Angie to take her up on it.

"Sure. Three o'clock is great," Angie said.

"See you then," Ree said, deciding this would keep things lighter and more social.

"Should I bring anything?" Angie asked.

"Just yourself," Ree said before walking over to talk to her "husband."

"HEY, BEAUTIFUL," QUINT SAID, before leaning forward and pressing a tender kiss on Ree's lips after she joined him in the weight room. The move was for show, and he'd done his best to be convincing. His body's reaction wasn't part of the plan. It wanted to haul her against his chest and do a whole lot more.

The cover was necessary so Quint wasn't busted staring at Mystery Guy, who seemed to be escorting Lola to the elevator.

"We're having company at three o'clock," Ree said, her emerald eyes sparkling a little more than usual. He blamed it on the lighting.

"Angie?" he asked.

"And Lola," she stated with more than a hint of pride in her voice.

"I'd rather have you to myself, honey." He kissed

her again. He threw out the line in case anyone was listening. There was a sprinkling of guys at the gym, all doing their own things with weights. One was in front of mirrors, grunting while powerlifting. Another was off to the other side on a machine. Give Quint a dumbbell set and a weight bench and he'd be good to go.

Mystery Guy and Lola took the elevator and disappeared from view a few moments later.

"You'll have to share me for a little while," she said, leaning into him. "But after work, I'm all yours."

"Promise?" he teased, trying to lighten the mood. The comment stirred emotions deep in his chest.

She leaned in and whispered, "Did you see him?"

"That sounds right up my alley," he said in a cryptic answer.

"Are they gone?" Her lips were so close to his ear he could feel her warm breath. It caused the hairs on his neck to stand at attention and blood to flow south.

"I'd definitely say yes to doing that later," he said, continuing the ruse in case they were being overheard or watched. As it was, they had Mystery Guy in the building and connected to their current case, and Lola was coming over at three o'clock. Good progress was being made already. His cell buzzed. He fished it out of his pocket.

There was a message from Lynn Bjorn, their boss. Call in fifteen minutes.

"Looks like my workout is over," Quint said, showing her the screen.

"I'll grab two waters before we head up," Ree said

with a smile before turning around and heading toward the small glass-door fridge.

Quint forced his gaze from her sweet backside, thinking he'd much rather do something else in fifteen minutes. A call from the boss at this stage of the investigation never signaled good news.

He toweled off and then wiped down the weights out of courtesy before following Ree to the elevator. The water was cold and refreshing going down his throat.

"I might not have been there long, but I managed to work up a decent sweat," he said.

"You're welcome to the shower first if you want," Ree said. "I can take mine after the call with your mother." Those last three words were for the couple's benefit who'd jumped in the elevator before the doors closed.

The guy was tall and somewhere in between Quint's and Ree's ages. He would guess closer to Ree's. The guy's—Quint performed a quick check for wedding bands and saw a matching set—wife was definitely closer to Ree's. The pair was opposite in pretty much every way. He was tall and she was short. He had sandy-blond hair whereas hers was a dark brown. His eyes were blue; hers were brown.

It wasn't until the pair got off the elevator on the fifth floor that Quint realized what was bothering him about the couple. He stifled a few choice words, waiting until they got inside their apartment before walking to the bedroom area to let a few rip.

"I saw it, too." Ree joined him, perching on the edge of the bed after grabbing a towel from the bathroom and folding it to presumably protect the bedspread from her sweat. "The haircut. The subtle way he walked with his right arm extended a little bit farther from his hip like he was used to a gun being there. What is other law enforcement doing in the building?"

"That has to be what the call with Bjorn is about," he said, flexing and releasing his fingers a few times to work off some of the tension that had been building since the text. "They might be unrelated to this case."

Ree shot him a look. "What are the odds of that happening?"

He put up a hand in surrender. This development sent his blood pressure soaring. Then there was the frustration this morning of not being able to place Mystery Guy from last night. Speaking of whom… "Did Lola say why Mystery Guy was in the building?"

"We didn't talk about him," she said. "I didn't even realize he was standing at the elevators until she walked away."

"I saw him when he came out of the elevator a few seconds before she turned around, but that was about it," he said.

"He must have known when her class would end," Ree pointed out as the cell phone in Quint's hand buzzed.

"Guess we're about to find out what the deal is with the other couple," he said before answering.

"I have news," Bjorn said. The fact that their boss was all business was another bad sign.

"I'm putting the call on speaker," Quint informed her before tapping the screen. "Ree is here with me."

"Good," Bjorn said. The sound of her issuing a sharp sigh came over the line. "I know this isn't going to go over very well, so I'll get straight to the point. The DEA is involved in the case, and we have agreed to cooperate."

Quint's blood pressure spiked again.

"Why is that?" he asked, clenching his back teeth to hold back from what he really wanted to say.

"We both know why the DEA would be involved," Bjorn said matter-of-factly. "Drugs."

"This complicates things," Quint said after a long, thoughtful pause.

"I know," Bjorn said.

Did she, though? Or had he become so good at hiding the truth that even his boss was blind to him?

Chapter Nine

Ree tucked a loose tendril of hair behind her ear as she studied the phone. Looking directly at Quint right now would only make matters worse. She heard the struggle in his tone of voice and knew exactly what this news would do to him. An investigation including multiple agencies would send him back to that place a little more than half a year ago where his partner was killed. Quint might ultimately blame himself for not forcing her to go to Bjorn, but the mistake came from multiple agencies rushing to a bust.

"Speak up, Agent Casey," their boss said.

"I'm here," he responded. "Just processing how to make this work."

Ree did glance up at that comment and saw the anguish in his eyes that belied the calmness in his tone. She reached out and touched him on the forearm, taking it as a bad sign that he immediately pulled his arm back like he'd just bumped into a lit burner. She took a second to consider her next move carefully. The option to request to be removed from the case would get her home to check on her grandfather. It would also leave

Quint stranded. They could come up with an excuse, and he could continue with the investigation. But she was the one with the job at the bar. Ree was already making inroads with Lola. It was only a matter of time before they figured out who Mystery Guy was now that Ree had an in with the bartender.

On the flip side, Quint was a talented agent. There was a reason he was considered the best to the point of having legendary status at work. He'd taken a big hit in losing his partner and best friend. The situation was sad from every angle. Was he over the loss? Probably not. Was he determined to find Dumitru and make him pay? Absolutely. This being personal for Quint raised the stakes of an already-dangerous assignment.

Still, she couldn't walk out on her partner. She knew it the minute she glanced over at him and they locked gazes. The slight nod she gave told him the answer he seemed to be searching for. His sigh of relief shouldn't make her want to walk over and loop her arms around his neck. And yet the kisses they'd shared sizzled like none other in her past, probably in her present and most definitely ever would in her future.

"Who is going to be our contact on the DEA side?" Ree asked, breaking the silence.

"That will be Nicholas Primer," Bjorn supplied. "We've worked with him before, and his team is top-notch."

"Sounds good." Ree grasped the sales job their boss was doing to soften the blow. Bjorn must realize how bad this was for Quint. He stood at the window, absently rubbing the stubble on his chin while engaged in what looked like deep thought.

"The details and contact information are uploaded to the case file," Bjorn said. The phone went quiet for a few long seconds. "Agent Casey."

"I'm here," he said after clearing his throat. He didn't turn away from the window, and Ree took that as a bad sign.

"You're good, right?" Bjorn asked.

"You saw my file. I've been cleared to work for months," he countered. "I passed all the psych evals you requested. Why would you be concerned about me now?"

"Good. That's what I wanted to hear." Bjorn sounded relieved. She wouldn't be if she was standing in the room. The tension thickened as Quint seemed to get lost inside his head.

"I'll check the file ASAP," Quint promised before lifting his elbow up against the window as he pinched the bridge of his nose like he was staving off a headache.

"Let me know if you have any questions or difficulties with any of Agent Primer's team," Bjorn said. She was lingering on the call like she was waiting for a definitive sign Quint was on board.

"We will," Ree finally spoke up. "Thanks for the information. We look forward to working with Agent Primer and his team."

Quint sucked in a breath but seemed able to hold his tongue as Ree ended the call.

"The couple from the elevator," he said through what

sounded like clenched teeth. "Let me guess…Agent Primer."

"We'll know when we open the file and see his picture. But, yes, I'm assuming the same thing," she said. When one of her brothers got in a mood like this, they were best left alone. A couple of days would pass and whatever they'd been angry about would blow over. Partnerships didn't work like that. She had to figure out a way to get Quint to speak to her.

He grunted as he stood there, staring.

"I know this probably brings back bad memories—"

"You don't know hell about what happened," he said, raising his voice. "And you don't know hell about what it cost me."

"No, Quint. I don't. But I will if you sit down and talk to me," she said evenly. "I can throw on a pot of coffee and we can move to the living room where we can talk like civilized adults."

Her words must've pushed the wrong buttons, because when she glanced over at him, his entire face was red.

"If you want a civilized adult, go talk to Agent Primer," he said, and his voice seethed.

"That's not fair and you know it," Ree countered, her own temperature rising to a level barely below boiling point. A few calming breaths brought her heat level down a couple of notches.

Quint, on the other hand, looked like a teakettle that was about to burst.

"Hey," she started, taking a softer tact. "You're right about one thing. I don't know." She paused to give those words a minute to sink in. "I don't know anything about what you went through or how it must have felt." Again, she paused. "All I can say is that I wish you'd talk to me and help me understand."

"It wouldn't bring her back," he said with so much anger the walls practically shook. "There's no use in dredging up bad memories."

Having grown up with four brothers, Ree knew a thing or two about when she'd lost a fight. This was one of those times. She pushed up to standing and grabbed the towel she'd been seated on.

"I'm going to take a shower, put on a pot of coffee and then open the file. Your choice as to whether or not you want to join me for two of those three things." With that, she made a beeline to the bathroom. She closed the door a little louder than she'd intended, and then turned on the spigot. Ten minutes later, she was clean and ready to face the other room.

Ree had no idea if Quint would even be there, let alone still in a sour mood, but time wasn't a luxury they had much of. Ree wanted to prep for the three o'clock with Lola. Then there was her shift tonight she had to mentally prepare for.

She walked out of the bathroom. At least Quint had left the spot at the window. He was probably gone, and that might be for the best. Let him cool off before they took another go at being civil with each other. Besides, seeing the pain in his eyes was a dagger to the heart and not something she was eager to get back to.

The smell of a fresh pot of coffee hit her the minute she turned left to head into the main living space. It was a welcome scent. Quint stood in the small kitchen with the light out. It was tucked inside the apartment near the door and fairly enclosed so as not to allow a lot of the natural light from the wall of windows inside.

"I made a cup and opened the file." He motioned toward the sofa, where the laptop sat on the coffee table, looking ready to go.

"I'll make one and join you," she said, but he shook his head. He filled a cup and handed it through the pass-through counter. "Thank you, Quint."

He didn't respond. Instead, he grunted and then walked over to the sofa.

QUINT SAT DOWN in front of the laptop. Ree joined him a few seconds later, sitting close enough for their outer thighs to touch as he opened the case file.

"Figures," she said, and then took a sip of coffee. Primer's face filled the left-hand side of the screen.

"Knew it," Quint said with a little more frustration than intended. Then again, the emotion seemed to be playing on repeat today.

"I'm guessing the female who was with him is also an agent," Ree said.

Quint clicked a couple of keys and brought up her picture next. "Chelle Mickelberg."

Ree sat back and scooted away from Quint. "Lola mentioned having a brother named Esteban. Do you think it's possible he's Mystery Guy?"

"It would make sense," Quint reasoned. "Her brother might know her schedule and need something from her."

"That would explain why he showed up after class today," she said. "They could be roommates, too."

"True," Quint agreed. "I'm not sure why the agency didn't tell us about a brother's possible involvement in her life."

"She mentioned that the two of them came to America together," Ree supplied. "It's possible he's living under the radar, possibly illegally."

"Grappell should be able to dig around and get an answer for us." Quint pulled up his email and then fired off a quick note to Agent Grappell. He was one of the best and having him on this case provided consistency, which went a long way in Quint's book. He would take all the wins he could get.

"What else?" Ree asked.

"Study the file on Primer," Quint said. "Looks like he's been decorated more than most professional athletes."

"A rising star at the DEA?" she asked, but the question was rhetorical, so Quint answered by way of another grunt.

They both realized what a pain a guy like that could be to have around. He sounded like the type who would want all the glory and most likely take credit for other people's work. Guys like that cared more about building a thick file of accolades and were usually all show and no substance.

"I should probably be the designated go-between on our side," Ree said.

"Are you afraid I can't keep my cool when I need to?" He twisted up his face.

To her credit, Ree maintained a calm but distant disposition. "Do I need to be?"

"No," he said dismissively.

"Good. Your answer doesn't change anything. I'll be the point person," she said. "Are you okay with that?"

He pulled up Primer's file and then turned the screen for her to see it. "His contact information is right there, but we should probably both have it just in case we aren't together when contact needs to be made."

"That's fair." She retrieved her cell phone and entered the information into her contacts. "Looks like he's going by the name Nick Driver."

"People pick whatever name is easiest to remember. Driver is close enough to Primer," Quint reasoned.

"He also kept his first name like we did," she added as she studied the screen. "Did you see this?" She pointed toward a line that indicated the agent would be working in the office of the bar as a new events and marketing manager.

"As long as he cooperates when necessary and stays out of our way when not, I don't care if he buys the place," Quint bit out. This complicated his infiltrating the office to be the computer guy. Randy, the owner, was on the up-and-up, but doing computer work would have given Quint a reason to hang around the bar more.

"If you can believe his file, he's one of the best at what he does," Ree said. She must have made the same assumptions about the agent based on her tone. "I'll reach out to him in a few minutes."

"The female agent, Chelle, is going by Shelly Driver," Quint pointed out.

"What does she do for a living according to her file?"

Quint scrolled down.

"Turns out, she's a yoga instructor," he said.

"Please tell me she doesn't work in the same building," Ree said on a sigh.

"It's bad enough they live here," he stated. "They could have moved into one of the other buildings on this block. But, no, she won't be working in the building. The studio where she's employed is on the same street as the bar."

"It must be close, then," she reasoned.

"That's probably a safe bet." He entered the studio address into Google Maps. "It's two doors down."

"Figures," she said. "You'll still be able to come to the bar for a nightcap. I can sell it as you going to school during the day while I sleep in after a long night of work."

"As long as it won't cast suspicion on you," he said.

"Lola remembered us from last night," Ree said, and he picked up something different in her tone.

"Speaking of her, we probably should have introduced ourselves at the bar. But it's fine. Right now, we should probably make lunch and get ready for her to drop by," he said.

"You're right about introducing ourselves that first night. I had the same thought but decided not to interrupt her. No going back to change it now," she said on a shrug. Little mistakes were expected on a case. They couldn't get too inside their heads about what they couldn't go back and fix. "I'll join you in a second. I want to order a few things to personalize the apartment."

"Suit yourself." Quint pushed up to standing. He still hadn't showered after working out, so he did that first. By the time he finished and hit the kitchen, Ree was done with her online shopping.

"It's wild that I literally just placed an order and the items will be delivered in—" she checked the time "—less than four hours."

"The benefits of city life," he said.

"I've lived my whole life in a small town," she said. "I travel all around the state for work now and have seen the benefits of urban living." She paused for a thoughtful moment. "At the end of the day, I don't need a lot to be happy. A cold drink, a little space between me and my neighbors, and a good book is all I need to be happy."

"No companionship?" he asked, wondering if she intended to spend the rest of her life alone.

"That's what the book is for," she said.

"Fair enough," he responded.

"How about you?" she asked, taking a seat on the barstool at the pass-through counter leading to the kitchen.

"What about me?" he asked, noting she'd turned the tables.

"What makes you happy?" she asked.

He resisted the temptation to say her, so he waved her off instead.

Chapter Ten

The DEA's involvement in the case could undermine the work Ree and Quint were putting in. Ree didn't like it one bit. The fact that it seemed to be a trigger for Quint wasn't helping matters. His body language had changed the second he heard the news. And if she was blind to that, anger practically radiated off him.

While he pulled together lunch, she reached out to Nick.

"No answer?" Quint's eyebrow came up in disapproval.

She left a message for Nick that was cryptic enough in the event it was intercepted and then nodded toward Quint. "I'm sure he'll get back to me when he can."

There were all kinds of reasons Nick might not have his phone with him in the apartment. But it could be a power play. His way of letting her know she wasn't a priority. In which case, he was a class A jerk, and working together was going to be real "fun."

A quick lunch of grocery store–prepared chicken salad on a lettuce leaf was enough to keep her stomach from growling. Before she knew it, there was a knock at the door.

Ree hopped up and checked the peephole. She opened the door and welcomed Angie inside. "What is that?"

"I made a little bowl of trail mix. I hope it's okay," Angie said. "It didn't seem right to show up empty-handed."

"Of course, it's great," Ree said, taking the large bowl. "Warm?"

"I like to pop mine in the oven and pour it into a warm bowl." Angie blushed. And then Ree realized why. Quint stepped into the entryway.

"You must be Angie," he said, sticking out his hand. "My name is Quint."

"I, um." Angie cleared her throat before continuing. She shook his hand, and her cheeks turned several shades darker. "Saw you down at the gym today. Nice to meet you."

"Any friend of my wife's is always welcome," he said, seemingly unaware of the effect he had on the opposite sex. Or maybe he was just so used to it that it no longer registered.

A twinge of jealousy pinched in the center of Ree's chest.

"I'll put this on the counter," she said.

"Thanks," Angie said, following Ree as Quint took his spot in the kitchen.

"Did you get any studying in today?" Ree asked.

Before Angie could answer, there was another knock at the door. Ree excused herself, checked the peephole, and then froze. What was Nick Driver doing standing on the other side of the door when he should have called first or returned her text?

Ree took a step back so she'd be in Quint's view, and then shook her head. The face she made should hopefully clue him in to the fact that this scenario was about to go downhill quick.

"Hey, honey, I asked a neighbor to borrow a couple of eggs," Quint said, maintaining a straight face while in full view of Angie, who'd taken a seat across from him.

A shot of adrenaline caused Ree's heart to pound. She cracked the door open and made a face that she hoped would tell Nick just how unwelcome he was at the moment.

The agent started to speak, but she shushed him, praying Angie couldn't hear. The young woman was a busybody. Quint started whistling, providing some background noise as cover.

"Thank you for the eggs," she said to the agent.

His eyebrows drew together before it seemed to dawn on him this wasn't a good time.

"Anytime," he said with a salute.

She mouthed the word *go*.

"Tell your husband to stop by when he has a chance," Nick said a little louder this time.

"Anything important I should pass along?" Ree asked.

"No. Just swinging by to say hello," the agent said with a scowl.

"Will do, then," Ree said before saying goodbye and

closing the door. She could only hope Angie hadn't caught on to the fact nothing had been handed over and Nick had no idea about the eggs.

Angie rounded the corner after Ree fisted her hands and before she made the "handoff" to Quint. The wall should have blocked their real activity from her view. Quint opened and closed the fridge.

"Who was that?" Angie asked.

"This new guy I met at the gym. His name is..." Quint pretended to draw a blank, which was smart when Ree thought about it, because now it could be anyone in the building.

"Is he on seven?" Angie asked. "Because I know everyone on our floor and some from others."

Before Quint could respond, another knock interrupted them.

"I'll get it," Ree said. She turned around and checked the peephole before opening the door again. "Lola, come on in. Angie just arrived as well."

Lola smiled as she entered the apartment. She had a laptop tucked under one arm and a bottle of wine in her free hand. She leaned in cheek to cheek and made a kissing noise as she greeted Ree warmly.

"I brought this for you and your husband." Lola held up the wine. "Welcome to the building and to Houstonian NightClub."

"You didn't have to bring us anything," Ree said, taking the bottle and stepping aside so Lola could greet Angie with the same warm acknowledgment.

"Please, it's nothing," Lola said with a small headshake. "A small gift."

Quint joined them, and another twinge of jealousy hit when Lola gave him the same treatment.

"I see you brought the offending piece of technology," Quint said.

Lola smiled. She seemed less affected by his looks, but she was probably hit on dozens of times a night by wealthy, good-looking men. Then there was Constantin, her boyfriend. A guy with the nickname Lights Out probably didn't like his girlfriend flirting with anyone else. She would have learned very quickly to hide any reactions she had to other men.

"Yes," she said. "I hope you can fix it. My boyfriend keeps telling me to buy a new one, but then it has to be set up again and I have all my pictures stored on this. I'm used to it and I know how it works."

"I'll give it a look and see what I can do," he said as she handed over the device.

"And I'll open this." Ree held up the bottle. "Four glasses?"

"I'm in," Angie said with a bounce.

Lola nodded.

"Honey?" Ree asked Quint. He moved to her and planted a tender kiss on her lips.

"If you're pouring, I'm drinking," he said with a wink. "Why don't you ladies take the living room and I'll work over here at the counter?"

Angie and Lola moved to the living room and took seats on the sofa while Ree located a corkscrew and then handed it and the bottle to Quint. She was fully capable of opening the bottle herself but had learned a long time ago the best way to get cooperation from others and disarm them was to show weakness in their presence.

Quint opened the bottle as Ree pulled out four glasses.

"Lucky us, they all match," she quipped, trying to shake off the heaviness of their earlier conversation and the near-miss of Nick showing up moments before Lola. As it was, Ree couldn't be 100 percent certain the two of them hadn't walked right past each other as she left the elevator and he got on. At least Lola hadn't seen him at Ree's door or questioned them about the agent.

Ree filled four glasses as Quint retrieved his laptop from the living room and set it next to Lola's on the counter.

"In case I need to look something up," he said.

"He's so good with those things," Ree said, setting a glass in front of him using the pass-through. She balanced two glasses in one arm and held the third in her free hand. Walking into the living room without spilling was a true testament to her ability to save every drop of a good wine.

"Password?" Quint asked over his shoulder. Lola shouted out something that sounded a lot like her birthday.

Ree sat on the plush rug opposite the bowl of treats and hoped Quint could get something from Lola's computer.

"THIS IS GREAT, THANKS," Quint said to Lola. Shock struck like a stray bullet when her wallpaper filled the screen. A kid who was the spitting image of Lola and looked to be about two and a half to three years old was the background for a cluttered desktop.

First things first, Quint organized her desktop. He moved icons into a new folder he created and marked *Stuff*.

"I need to run a diagnostic tool," he said aloud, but he doubted anyone heard him over Angie's laughter and the buzz of conversation. Ree's opening the bottle of wine was a brilliant move. There was plenty of time for the drink to wear off before her shift, and it might loosen up Lola and Angie.

Quint grabbed the flash drive he'd set out in case he got the chance to use it and plugged it in. Thankfully, she didn't have an Apple product since they did away with regular USB ports a while ago, and that would have made this job a whole lot more difficult.

As he copied her hard drive, he poked around on her device. There wasn't much more than an endless number of pictures of her kid, and Constantin. The ones with Constantin only went back a year or so, giving Quint the impression the kid didn't belong to him. She seemed to mainly use her PC for surfing the web and shopping. She kept way too many tabs open, so he closed all of those. Her battery was low.

"I'm guessing the power cord is at your place," Quint said.

"Yes," Lola said, turning to look at him. "Do you need me to go get it?" She started to get up, but he waved her off.

"I have enough power to get by, but you should think about replacing the battery if you want to keep this laptop around. Keep it charged between ten and ninety percent for optimal life," he stated, figuring he needed to throw out a few facts for credibility's sake. He was also doing his best to distract himself from the fact that Nick had shown up after Ree called and left a message. It was exactly the kind of thing that could make a case go haywire, and he planned on having a few choice words with the DEA agent when the time was right. The incident was also going in Quint's report. Normally, he would cover for anyone and have a fellow agent's back. If this guy was as great as his file would have everyone believe, he should have known better than to pay a surprise visit.

When the files were finished copying over to the flash drive, Quint pulled it out and set it to the side.

"I noticed you have virus protection software installed," Quint said to Lola.

"Isn't that a good thing?" she asked.

"No. No." He shook his head. "It's the first place hackers look."

"I thought it was the opposite. It has a shield," she said.

"The software keeps a back door on your system for any experienced computer nerd to walk through. I'm removing it now," he said.

"Won't that leave the front door open?" she asked. Good analogy.

"I'll build a custom firewall," he said. "It'll be the best way to protect what's inside."

She nodded and said, "Ahhh, okay. That sounds much smarter."

Quint was finished uninstalling her so-called virus protection software and the firewall was up in less than fifteen minutes. "Normally, when a computer just shuts down by itself it's overheating, it has battery problems, the heat sink fan is being temperamental or there's a virus."

"It sounds like I've been holding the door open for a virus," she said. "Maybe that's what is happening?"

"It's possible. It might take a few minutes to check." He downloaded virus-scanning software before adding, "The most likely culprit for something like this would be bad RAM. It's swappable, but let's hope it's a battery issue. That's easier to replace."

"Do batteries just do this?" she asked, leaning in his direction.

"If the battery can't give consistent voltage due to it being old or having something like water damage, then the laptop will shut off," he informed.

"Water damage is possible. I sometimes have it open in the kitchen when I'm using it for a recipe," she said. "My kitchen is the same size as yours."

"That might explain it," he surmised. "I'll order a new battery and have it delivered to your place."

"I'm in nine-three, same as you. The only difference is the floor," she said with a proud smile. Looking at her now, he realized she reminded him of the famous actress Penélope Cruz. He would mention it to Ree later.

He ordered a new battery for Lola to be delivered to her place. The convenience of online ordering would provide her with a brand-new battery tomorrow. He had to give it to Houston, it had the online ordering and delivery operation down pat. He also thought about Constantin and his truck business. How easy would it be to slip trucks in and out of the city along with all the home deliveries going on? Pretty damn easy.

Glancing over at Lola, seeing her quiet strength, he wondered how she'd ended up in a relationship with someone like Constantin. Looks could be deceiving, Quint knew firsthand, and yet she didn't seem the type to be involved with the criminal element.

The round, angelic face beaming at him from the computer might explain why she worked at the bar. She could work nights while the kid slept. She must have someone to help with mornings considering the fact that she was at Pilates this morning. There was no kid in sight now. Did she have a live-in babysitter?

The computer dinged, indicating it was finished with the scan, as Quint took a sip of the wine. He checked the screen. There were two suspicious apps he could uninstall, and one he figured he should leave in. But how did he tell her someone had installed spyware on her laptop?

Chapter Eleven

Ree glanced over at Quint. From his profile, she could see that he'd found something he didn't like on Lola's computer.

"Who needs a refill?" Ree asked, draining her glass of wine. It gave her a good reason to get up.

"Yes, please," Angie said, hoisting her glass.

"I'll take one as well," Lola stated with a smile. She had a warmth to her that made it so difficult to believe she would be involved with criminals. It was a real shock to think she was in a relationship with someone like Constantin.

"I'll be right back." Ree set her glass down on the coffee table, figuring it would be best to bring the bottle to the conversation. Angie was a good conversationalist and kept Lola engaged while Ree retrieved the bottle from the kitchen. There was enough inside to cover three of them. Ree had only half filled the glasses earlier since it was before dinnertime and most people objected to a heavy first-round pour. Get one glass in them, and they usually lightened up on the refill.

Ree palmed the bottle, wishing she could ask Quint

what was going on. He turned toward her when his back was to the others and shot a look that confirmed she saw what she thought she did. There'd been a discovery.

Heading back into the living room, she also saw the intensity in his eyes. She'd seen it for the first time in Cricket Creek during much of the investigation there. He'd finally started letting his guard down by the end of the investigation. Bringing another agency into the case caused a few more walls to come up between them.

"So, Lola, who was the hottie at the elevator today?" Angie finally asked. The younger woman's cheeks were a darker shade of pink, indicating she was probably a little tipsy.

"No one important." Lola shook off the comment. "Plus, where is your fireman today?"

"We have yet to meet him," Ree added. Lola shot a look that said she appreciated the distraction.

"At work," Angie said. "Y'all, the man is always at work." This was the most Southern Angie had been since they'd met. Ree cracked a smile at the slip. Apparently, a little afternoon wine brought out the South in Angie.

"Probably makes it easier to hide him from your parents," Ree pointed out.

"They would kill me if they knew," Angie said before taking another sip and smiling like a kid who'd just gotten away with eating the last cookie from the jar and no one knew who did it.

"Why not just sit them down and have a talk?

You're..." Ree drew her eyebrows together. "How old did you say?"

"Twenty-two," Angie announced. "The problem is that they're paying for my apartment."

"What about Mr. Fireman?" Lola asked.

"He moved in with me because I refused to live with him. He was in a house with four other guys and the place smelled like stale beer and pizza," she said, wrinkling her nose.

"Do you really want to spend the rest of your life with a slob?" Lola asked with a look of sheer disgust.

It made Ree laugh.

"Sorry," she said to Lola, "but your face just cracked me up."

"Y'all, my guy is clean. It's half the reason he was ready to move out, but he's still in a lease until the end of October, so he pays for the other place and we live here," Angie said. "It bothers him to no end that my family doesn't know he lives here. He's been threatening to tell them the next time he sees them. Says we're living a lie."

"He sounds like a really stand-up guy to me," Ree said with compassion and a whole new respect for the fireman.

"If you don't hurry up and marry that guy, I will," Lola teased. A ringtone sounded and she immediately reached into her handbag. "Excuse me." She practically jumped up as she pulled out her cell. After checking the screen, she immediately moved toward the door.

"Hello," she answered as she headed into the hallway. The rest of the conversation was out of earshot.

Angie locked gazes with Ree and made a face. Ree shrugged.

"She sure hightailed it out of here quick," Angie said.

"I hope everything's okay," Ree commented. She checked the clock before polishing off her glass of wine. "I have to be at work in an hour and a half."

"At your new job?" Angie's lips compressed like she was struggling to hold back a laugh.

"I know. It's probably bad form, but I'll just eat some more of this amazing trail mix to soak up the alcohol and I'll be fine." Ree shifted the lighthearted conversation with Angie.

A minute later, Lola came back inside. Her shoulders were rounded, and it looked like someone had deflated the air in her chest. All confidence was gone.

"Everything okay?" Ree asked as she and Angie turned their attention to Lola.

She held up her phone and apologized. "I forgot about a meeting that I have with a friend. It's stupid of me."

"I'll have your laptop ready in a few seconds," Quint said. He turned to look at her when she didn't immediately respond. "Is that okay? Because I can stop the scanning process right now and hand it over if you need to go."

"Five minutes is probably enough time, right?" she asked.

"I can make that work," he said. "It's just doing its thing right now, searching for any additional problems." He hesitated like he was engaged in an internal debate.

Then he leaned toward Lola and quietly said, "There is something I should probably show you on here."

"Oh?" Her voice rose a couple of octaves, and she seemed to realize this wasn't going to be good news.

"See this." He pointed to the screen, but Ree couldn't see what he was referring to from her spot on the living room floor.

She tucked her feet underneath her bottom and grabbed another handful of the snack. "This is so amazing. What all is in here?"

Angie had been staring at Lola. The younger woman cleared her throat and started listing off the ingredients. While she did, she stared at the bowl.

"This is called spyware," Quint explained so low Ree had to strain to hear him.

"What's that exactly?" Lola asked, sounding a little put off.

"It's probably what you think it is. It's a way for someone to access your computer remotely," he explained quietly.

"Like, they don't have to be in the room?" she asked.

"They don't even have to be in the building," he stated. "This program will allow the person on the other end to read your emails and see what websites you're on."

Lola exhaled a slow breath.

"Thank you for telling me," she said.

"I didn't touch it. Whoever installed this would know if I blocked access," he said.

"I see." Lola's shoulders straightened and her back

was now ramrod straight. Chin up, she said, "I appreciate knowing what is happening."

"I just thought you should be aware," he said with a whole lot of compassion and sympathy.

She nodded, and even from the adjacent room it was easy to see she was trying to hold back tears.

"And pretzels," Angie said proudly.

"Without them, it wouldn't be this addictive." Ree rejoined the conversation. Was Lola really so naive that she didn't think her criminal boyfriend would keep tabs on her? Based on her reaction to the news, the answer was yes. Was it possible Lola had no idea Constantin was a criminal?

More questions joined those when Ree saw the sweet, angelic face fill the screen as Quint closed down the program scanning for more viruses. Turned out, the real cancer was Constantin. In Lola's life? On Lola's computer? On society.

Worse yet, was he the father of her child?

"I BETTER GO. Thank you for everything," Lola said to Quint.

He'd debated keeping the information to himself, but her reaction told him a whole lot about the state of her relationship with Constantin. He closed out the window running the scan when it was finished, and then handed over her laptop. "You have a beautiful kid there."

"Thank you," Lola said with a smile that would warm the room in a freeze. "Lili is my life."

There was something about the way she said those last few words mixed with the wistful look on her face that made him realize she would do anything for that kid. Possibly even stay in a relationship that was no good for her.

Angie said her goodbyes as she followed Lola out the door after Quint handed over the laptop. Lola thanked him more times than necessary for his help. She turned to Ree.

"I'll see you later tonight," Lola said.

"See you soon," Ree stated.

Ree cleaned up the dishes in the living room before setting the half-empty trail mix bowl in front of him. Neither spoke until they heard Angie's door close and the elevator ding.

"I'm just going to check," Ree whispered as she walked over to the peephole. Her silence had him curious as to what was going down in the hall. It took a solid minute for the elevator to ding again, and then Ree came around the corner. "She stood in front of our door like she was contemplating knocking."

"I wasn't sure if it was a good idea to tell her about the spyware or not," he admitted. "She might have wanted to come back to ask questions."

"She needed to know," she said. "But I did see how shocked she was when you told her."

"It was the last thing she expected to hear," he agreed.

"Do you think it's possible she doesn't know what line of work Constantin is in?" Ree took the seat next to him. She seemed careful to keep her leg to her side, ensuring there was no incidental physical contact.

"It's hard to say," he stated.

"Maybe she'll start questioning her relationships more," Ree surmised.

He nodded as he inserted the flash drive into his laptop. "We got lucky that she doesn't have a MacBook."

"I'm guilty of the same thing," Ree said. Her expression was all business now when it came to him. It was probably for the best this way. Keep everything professional and not blur the lines, because it was quicksand—easy to step into and impossible to get out.

He pulled up the picture of Lola's child. "What do you think the chances are Constantin is this kid's father?"

"How old would you say this kid is?" Ree asked, studying the photo.

"Two and a half to three years," he said.

"Okay," she said, nodding. "Lola has only been in the country for two years. A pregnancy lasts nine months, so that means she would have known the guy three to four years ago when she was still in Argentina."

"Constantin is Romanian, so the odds he would have been in Argentina seem slim," Quint reasoned. "I'll send Grappell another email to ask how far back our intel goes to see if there's a chance he was in South America. He did just send an address for a warehouse not too far from here associated with the company All Transport. Said we might want to check it out."

"Okay. Duly noted." Something else caused her stance to shift, soften.

"I know we're supposed to follow the facts and not

let personal beliefs or intuition cloud our judgment, but I really don't want Lola to be like one of those jerks."

"There's a quality to her that makes it feel impossible to me, too," he said.

"It would be hard to fool both of us," she reasoned.

"All we can do is keep ourselves open to both possibilities," he finally said.

"Agreed," she said before glancing at the time. "Holy hell, I have to get ready for work."

"While you do that, I'll see what I can find on the flash drive," he said.

"You didn't install spyware on her system, did you?" Ree asked as she stood up and then pushed the chair in.

"No. Whoever installed the spyware in the first place knows enough about computers to make it dangerous for me to take that route. I just copied everything," he said.

"Right. That's smart," she said.

"Thank you," he responded, figuring he'd take all the compliments he could get at this point. As it was, he felt like a jerk for his reactions earlier. There was no reason to take out his frustration about working with another agency on Ree.

He needed to remind himself of the fact every chance he got, because he'd picked up on the distrust in her eyes since the phone call with Bjorn.

Quint clicked on the mail icon. It was password-protected. He figured Lola would use the same one as before, the one that unlocked her computer and felt like a birthday. He tapped his fingers on the counter as he tried to recall the numbers. They came to him after a few seconds. He entered the numbers *0424*.

The mail opened and filled his screen. Could he get the answers they sought there?

Chapter Twelve

Ree applied light makeup and fixed her auburn hair, slicking it to one side in a low side pony. Her uniform would be waiting at work, so she dressed in her interview outfit from the Cricket Creek job that was still packed in her overnight bag. She'd washed it and then thrown it back inside the bag with the rest of her clothes from the trip. The suitcase had never made it back into the closet, and the clothes never made it back into drawers. Turned out to be handy when this case popped up out of nowhere.

Not exactly out of nowhere. She'd half expected a call at some point asking if she'd like to join Quint. What she hadn't anticipated was him showing up at her mother's door. That had taken guts. It had shown his determination to work with her again on this case since he was willing to put himself in a situation where he wouldn't be welcomed.

She buttoned her white blouse, thinking the high but fashionable collar might be a mistake in this heat. She'd try not to end up soaked with sweat before she walked inside the bar. The high-waisted forest green pants fit well enough to show off the long legs she'd worked hard to tone at the gym. The cuffs struck just above her ankles, and black spiked heels added a couple of inches to her decent height. No one would accuse her of towering over anyone, but with good heels she could almost look someone who was six feet tall square in the eyes.

"Ready or not, here I come," she said as she joined Quint at the counter. He was in the exact spot where she last saw him, studying the screen.

He leaned back and turned to look at her. His eyes widened when he said, "Damn."

"What?" She could feel the red blush crawling up her neck again at the way he looked at her with appreciation in his eyes.

"You look beautiful" was all he said.

"This is the same outfit I wore at the cabin that first day," she reminded him.

"Then I was a jerk for not saying it when we first met," he said.

"I think you were busy defending yourself from the demands I was placing on you," she said with a half smile. She'd gone in like gangbusters on that first day.

Quint smirked. "Standing up for yourself is sexy."

Well, now Ree really didn't know what to say.

"I have to go. Did you find anything on there?" She motioned toward his laptop, needing to change the subject. His compliment didn't change the fact that a wall had come up between them or the challenges they faced working with the other agents.

"She's squeaky-clean so far," he said. "But then, most criminals are good about hiding their activities."

Quint closed the laptop and stood up. "I did get her daughter's birthday, though. April twenty-fourth."

"That helps," Ree said. "Ready?"

"Always," he said.

"Will you be coming in for a drink later?" she asked as they walked toward the door.

"I'll skip it tonight since it's your first shift," he said.

"Okay." She hid her disappointment. "I'll text you when I know what time I should be done."

Quint opened the door, and then held it for her as she walked past. She thanked him as she headed toward the elevator bank. There was something nice about chivalry not being dead. She pushed the elevator button and led the way toward HNC. The heat practically melted her, but at least her hair was off her neck. The collar turned out to be a bad idea even though Quint reassured her that she still looked beautiful as he turned her in at the door.

For show, he kissed her until her toes curled. A growing part of her wished those kisses meant something besides work. The logical side of her brain kicked in, reminding her that office romances had about as much of a chance of working out as spring flowers did of budding in December.

"See you back here when your shift is over," he said, leaning his forehead against hers like he needed a minute to gather his thoughts after the kiss. A self-satisfied smirk upturned the corners of her lips. Thank the heavens she wasn't the only one affected every time their lips touched.

"You two should be more careful or your agency might think something is really going on between you." Nick Driver's voice cut into the moment and his tone struck a nerve.

Quint pulled back and they both glanced around to make certain no one else heard the snide comment. Ree half expected Quint to speak up, but his jaw muscle clenched instead.

"Uncool," Quint said low and under his breath. Nick kept walking, unfazed.

"Later it is," she said to Quint, trying to pull his attention back to her before turning and walking in the door. She glanced back in time to see him standing there, arms folded.

Ree checked in with the shift manager, Julian, before getting her locker assignment and uniform. She changed in the back room and tucked her clothes and purse into the locker before securing it closed. The lock had one of those dials on it like a safe. She memorized her combination but was reassured the shift manager had a master key in the event Ree blanked out on what she'd been told.

Randy, the owner, had arranged for Ree to be Lola's barback. She walked over to the bar where Lola was bent down and arranging something on a shelf behind the bar. Ree brought over a tray of clean glasses and cleared her throat on the approach so as not to surprise Lola.

"I'm not ready," Lola said, her voice cracked.

"Okay, I'll come back," Ree said, turning with the heavy tray hoisted on her shoulder.

"Ree?" Lola glanced over but didn't stand up. Her eyes were red and puffy, and it looked like she'd been crying. She squatted down and grabbed a roll of paper towels, pulling off one and blotting her eyes with it. "Don't leave. I didn't realize it was you."

"I can give you a few minutes," Ree said, hating that Lola was upset but secretly hoping this might be the in Ree needed to get the bartender to open up about her personal life. It was good for the investigation, but Ree also wanted to know if she could still trust her own instincts.

"No. No. Don't be silly. That tray must weigh a hundred pounds." Lola waved Ree in.

Ree set the tray down on the countertop. It was filled with highball glasses, and the tray of expensive crystal probably cost more than a month of Ree's salary. "Where do these go?"

"Right here." Lola pointed toward a shelf just under the lip of the bar and within easy reach.

"Are you okay?" Ree asked, scooting the tray down as she moved closer to Lola.

"Yes, but please don't let Julian see me like this," Lola pleaded, blotting her eyes again. "He doesn't like anyone to bring drama to work."

"Okay." Ree was almost finished putting away the last of the glasses when Julian turned and headed toward them. She smiled and said out of the side of her mouth, "He's coming over here."

"That's no good. He'll fire me, and I need this job."

Treat Yourself
with 2 Free Books!

Suspense

Suspenseful Romance

GET UP TO 4 FREE BOOKS &
2 FREE GIFTS WORTH OVER $20

See Inside For Details

Claim Them While You Can

Get ready to relax and indulge with your FREE BOOKS and more!

Claim up to FOUR NEW BOOKS & TWO MYSTERY GIFTS – absolutely FREE!

Dear Reader,

We both know life can be difficult at times. That's why it's important to treat yourself so you can relax and recharge once in a while.

And I'd like to help you do this by sending you this amazing offer of up to FOUR brand new full length FREE BOOKS that WE pay for.

This is everything I have ready to send to you right now:

Try **Harlequin® Romantic Suspense** books featuring heart-racing page-turners with unexpected plot twists and irresistible chemistry that will keep you guessing to the very end.

Try **Harlequin Intrigue® Larger-Print** books featuring action-packed stories that will keep you on the edge of your seat. Solve the crime and deliver justice at all costs.
Or TRY BOTH!

All we ask in return is that you answer 4 simple questions on the attached Treat Yourself survey. You'll get **Two Free Books** and **Two Mystery Gifts** from each series you try, *altogether worth over $20*! Who could pass up a deal like that?

Sincerely,

Pam Powers

Harlequin Reader Service

Treat Yourself to Free Books and Free Gifts.

Answer 4 fun questions and get rewarded.

	YES	NO
1. I LOVE reading a good book.	◯	◯
2. I indulge and "treat" myself often.	◯	◯
3. I love getting FREE things.	◯	◯
4. Reading is one of my favorite activities.	◯	◯

TREAT YOURSELF • Pick your 2 Free Books...

Yes! Please send me my Free Books from each series I select and Free Mystery Gifts. I understand that I am under no obligation to buy anything, as explained on the back of this card.

Which do you prefer?
- ❏ **Harlequin® Romantic Suspense** 240/340 HDL GRCZ
- ❏ **Harlequin Intrigue® Larger-Print** 199/399 HDL GRCZ
- ❏ **Try Both** 240/340 & 199/399 HDL GRDD

FIRST NAME

LAST NAME

ADDRESS

APT.#

CITY

STATE/PROV.

ZIP/POSTAL CODE

EMAIL ❏ Please check this box if you would like to receive newsletters and promotional emails from Harlequin Enterprises ULC and its affiliates. You can unsubscribe anytime.

▶ DETACH AND MAIL CARD TODAY! ▶

HI/HRS-520-TY22

🍁 **HARLEQUIN** Reader Service —**Here's how it works:**

Accepting your 2 free books and 2 free gifts (gifts valued at approximately $10.00 retail) places you under no obligation to buy anything. You may keep the books and gifts and return the shipping statement marked "cancel." If you do not cancel, approximately one month later we'll send you more books from the series you have chosen, and bill you at our low, subscribers-only discount price. Harlequin® Romantic Suspense books consist of 4 books each month and cost just $4.99 each in the U.S. or $5.74 each in Canada, a savings of at least 13% off the cover price. Harlequin Intrigue® Larger-Print books consist of 6 books each month and cost just $5.99 each for in the U.S. or $6.49 each in Canada, a savings of at least 14% off the cover price. It's quite a bargain! Shipping and handling is just 50¢ per book in the U.S. and $1.25 per book in Canada*. You may return any shipment at our expense and cancel at any time — or you may continue to receive monthly shipments at our low, subscribers-only discount price plus shipping and handling. *Terms and prices subject to change without notice. Prices do not include sales taxes which will be charged (if applicable) based on your state or country of residence. Canadian residents will be charged applicable taxes. Offer not valid in Quebec. Books received may not be as shown. All orders subject to approval. Credit or debit balances in a customer's account(s) may be offset by any other outstanding balance owed by or to the customer. Please allow 3 to 4 weeks for delivery. Offer available while quantities last. **Your Privacy** – Your information is being collected by Harlequin Enterprises ULC, operating as Harlequin Reader Service. For a complete summary of the information we collect, how we use this information and to whom it is disclosed, please visit our privacy notice located at https://corporate.harlequin.com/privacy-notice. From time to time we may also exchange your personal information with reputable third parties. If you wish to opt out of this sharing of your personal information, please visit www.readerservice.com/consumerschoice or call 1-800-873-8635. **Notice to California Residents** – Under California law, you have specific rights to control and access your data. For more information on these rights and how to exercise them, visit https://corporate.harlequin.com/california-privacy.

▲ If offer card is missing write to: Harlequin Reader Service, P.O. Box 1341, Buffalo, NY 14240-8531 or visit www.ReaderService.com ▲

BUSINESS REPLY MAIL
FIRST-CLASS MAIL   PERMIT NO. 717   BUFFALO, NY

POSTAGE WILL BE PAID BY ADDRESSEE

HARLEQUIN READER SERVICE
PO BOX 1341
BUFFALO NY 14240-8571

NO POSTAGE
NECESSARY
IF MAILED
IN THE
UNITED STATES

Lola said a couple of words in Spanish that Ree was pretty certain most sailors would understand.

"Julian, I have a question about something in my locker." Ree artfully moved herself out from behind the bar and toward the back room. All she could do was buy Lola a little more time to pull herself together.

Julian took the bait, looking like he genuinely wanted to help. Of course, it probably didn't hurt matters that Randy had personally hired her. Julian had to know he was out of his league with her. The fact that he seemed eager to help when he scowled at quite a few of the other employees told her that he treated Randy hires more nicely.

"I really couldn't figure out if I'd closed and locked this correctly," she said, feigning helplessness while stuffing down the frustration that she hadn't been able to come up with anything better off the top of her head and on short notice.

Julian tried the metal handle that shifted up like her old high school locker. The one she never used because she went to a large high school that had A/B days, rendering the locker useless.

"It didn't open, so looks like you're good," he said with what looked like a forced smile.

"Good. Thank you," she said, figuring she needed to come up with another question or two in order to stall him. "How many people will we have on the floor tonight?"

"It's Monday, so we can expect half the crowd we normally get. I scale down the number of employees accordingly so we don't waste money," Julian said.

He seemed especially proud of his answer as his chest puffed out just a little bit when he spoke. It signaled that he took pride in his work, which was always a good thing. How would he react if he knew the girlfriend of one of the biggest area weapons runners worked behind his bar?

Would he care as long as she showed up for work and kept customers happy?

"That's really smart," she said, trying to play up to his ego.

It worked. He practically beamed. He also probably figured she'd be reporting back to Randy.

"Do I get another uniform or should I plan on washing this one every night?" she asked.

"You'll get two," he said.

"Okay, great." An heir and a spare, she thought.

"Your size is popular, so the reason you have only one is because the other is on back order," he said. "Let me know if you need a day off in between shifts in order to have time to do a wash."

"I can take care of that easily," she said before shifting her weight to one side. "I just want to say that I can't thank you enough for this job. It means a lot to my family."

Julian swatted empty air.

"You'll be an asset to the company," he said.

She highly doubted most barbacks were treated this well.

"As soon as an opening for waitress comes up, I want you to know I'll be looking to you to possibly fill it," he said. Now he really was laying it on thick.

"I don't want to skip the line if someone else deserves it," she quickly said.

"No trouble at all. It'll go to the person best suited
for the job," he explained as someone yelled his name.
He spun around. "I better go see what that's about."

"Of course," she said, hoping she'd bought Lola
enough time to dry her eyes and throw on a little
makeup to cover the redness. She returned to her station to find Lola on her feet, wiping down the bar and
whistling as she worked. If Ree didn't know better, she
would have no idea that Lola had been crouching behind the bar crying ten minutes ago.

"Thank you," Lola said as Ree took her place, fin-
ishing putting away the last of the glasses.

"Anytime," Ree said, and really meant it.

QUINT'S SPANISH WAS a little too rusty to decipher all of
Lola's emails, so he uploaded the contents of her hard
drive to the case file on the database. There were lin-
guistic specialists who could take it from there. Using
Google's translator, he was able to get the gist of anything that drew his eye. So far, Lola came out clean.
There was also a computer specialist who would dis-
sect everything else. It had taken Quint the better part
of the night, but Ree's text that the bar was about to
close came just before midnight. She'd said it would
take only fifteen minutes to finish breaking down since
the night had been slow and everyone had pitched in to
make closing go as smoothly as possible.

Nick Driver was still on Quint's mind. He needed to
be made aware of just how uncool the stunt he'd pulled

was and how little a repeat would be tolerated. At the very least, it was unprofessional not to respond to Ree's text and then show up at the door. Then there was the snide comment in front of the bar. Quint's hands were tied on how to get the message across. He couldn't confront the guy or shoot a note to Bjorn to complain. She was already on high alert when it came to Quint working in cooperation with another agency.

Quint would sit on it for a while and see if any ideas turned up. He also didn't want to undermine Ree, who had agreed to be the go-between. By the time he exited his building and made the walk to HNC, Ree was standing out front with Lola.

"Hi, honey," Ree said, walking over to him and rising up to give him a kiss. He dipped his head and met her halfway. The kiss caused his pulse to skyrocket. It was strange, because he was usually used to kissing a fellow agent by the time they worked together on a second assignment. This shouldn't be any different. Driver's earlier comment sat heavy on Quint.

"Hey," he said, hearing the gravelly quality to his own voice. At least his reaction to her made the whole newlywed cover seem far more credible. He would leave it at that.

"We started to head home but decided to wait for you here in case you came from a different direction," Ree said. She glanced over at Lola. "Thank you for sticking around with me."

"No problem," Lola said, checking her phone. "It's what we do for each other, right?"

Ree's smile could light a city block during a blackout.

A Lamborghini roared up on the road next to them. Lola caught Ree's gaze. "Looks like my ride finally showed."

"See you tomorrow?" Ree asked.

"Tuesday's my night off," Lola said, rushing toward the vehicle like her life depended on it. She climbed in the passenger seat and shot a quick smile at Ree, who waved.

"I'm worried about her," Ree said as Quint linked their fingers. There was something right about holding Ree's hand. It made him feel like his demons might stay at bay for a while.

"How was your first night?" He needed to redirect the conversation to something a newlywed would ask as he turned them toward their building and started the walk back.

"It was good. I didn't make a lot of money, but it wasn't busy. Lola trained me throughout the night and we fell into a good rhythm. Julian sent most everyone home early. He let me stay since I'm new," she said.

"Makes sense," he said as they fell in step together.

"Everything was wiped down half an hour before closing," she said, leaning into him. The move was for show, but a small piece of him hoped it meant she'd forgiven him for how he'd acted toward her after the call with Bjorn.

"Sounds like it was a good way to get your feet wet before the weekend crowd hits," he said.

"That's why I don't get a day off this week," she said. "Julian thinks I'll be better off learning over the next few days before business picks up."

"I can't imagine what a Friday or Saturday night looks like when Sunday was as crowded as it was," he said as they reached the building.

"Apparently, the crowds start on Thursdays," she said.

"Doesn't anybody have to wake up early the next morning for work?" he mused.

"I guess not," she said as they entered the glass elevators. Almost the minute she stepped inside the apartment, the shoes came off. She kicked them beside the door with a groan. "Heels are definitely harder on the feet than boots."

"How do you wear those all night?" he asked.

"Practice, but that doesn't mean it feels good," she said, heading over to the sofa and plopping down in her work clothes. Her gaze flew to the boxes stacked neatly on the opposite side of the sofa. "My order came?"

"As promised," he said.

"I'm way too tired to open those boxes tonight. It'll give me something to do first thing in the morning," she said.

"Do you want Coke or something stronger?" he asked.

"Stronger," she said. "Definitely stronger."

Quint poured her a glass of wine and opened a beer for himself. One drink wouldn't hurt either one of them and after learning the DEA was on the case, Quint could use something to help him relax. He almost laughed out loud at the thought. A twelve-pack wouldn't make a dent in how frustrated and stressed he was and had been all day. Having a drink with Ree was the best part of his night so far.

Chapter Thirteen

"When I got to work, Lola was behind the bar crying," Ree informed Quint as she took the glass of wine from him. Their fingers brushed, and she was comforted by the familiar jolt of electricity.

"Did she say why?" he asked as the sofa dipped underneath his weight.

She tucked her feet underneath her bottom as she turned toward him. "She told me that she got in a fight with Lili's father."

"Mystery Guy?" he asked.

"He now has a name, too," she confirmed with a nod. "Matias Gimenez."

"Does he live here in the States?" he asked.

"He followed her and is demanding custody of Lili," Ree said.

"That wouldn't fly over here, but it could happen in Argentina," Quint stated. And then it seemed to dawn on him. "That's the reason she came here two years ago, isn't it?"

"We didn't get that far in our conversation with

Julian around, but that's my guess as well," she confirmed.

"I need to send Grappell the name and get a background check on Gimenez," Quint said before retrieving his laptop. He sent the note while she enjoyed the click-click-clack of the keyboard and the wine.

"There," he said before closing the laptop.

"Lola seems like a decent person. I'm not sure why she would let herself get mixed up with someone like Constantin. Matias doesn't exactly give me good vibes, either," she said.

"Women are attracted to powerful men. It's biology," he said.

"I'd like to think we've evolved from the caveman days," she said with a grunt of disapproval.

"No doubt we have. But biology takes a while to catch up," he said before taking a sip of beer. "What about Nick Driver?" Quint's jaw muscle ticked when he mentioned the DEA agent's name.

"No one mentioned him and, after our exchange, I didn't ask about him," she said. "He's supposed to work in the office, so I'm guessing that means only during the day." She drew her eyebrows together and frowned. "Right?"

"I believe so, unless there's an event at night. You'll have to attempt contact again if you want to find out. Hopefully, he'll start to upload his notes to the file we are supposed to make important case notes in," he said. "So far, it's empty in there."

"I'm not giving him my information on Lola," she argued.

"No one in this room would ask you to," Quint said without hesitation. His response came so fast she didn't have a ready comeback. "Meetings with him are too risky with a nosy neighbor and these paper-thin walls."

"I agree." Ree sent a text to Driver, asking if he found out anything he'd like to share, and waited for a response. None came.

"Should I be surprised by this at this point?" she asked, holding up the cell.

"Probably not, but we have to keep trying if only to appease Bjorn," Quint stated. "I'm not sure where she got her intel about him, but he doesn't strike me as co-operative so far."

"What about the laptop?" she asked after agreeing.

"I didn't find anything we can use. She seems on the straight and narrow," he said.

"Which makes even less sense why she would get herself involved with Constantin," she repeated. "I sound like a broken record, don't I?"

"You're just reasoning through it. I agree with you, by the way," he said. "Especially after peeking into her laptop. It was nothing but check-ins with her mother from what Google Translate could tell. I really should have paid more attention in high school Spanish class."

"Same." Ree broke into a smile. "I did find out why Matias was at the taco place last night. Lola asked him to stop by there on his way to the bar and bring her a couple of number twos. She said her boyfriend hadn't left the bar yet and she didn't want a scene. The delay tactic almost didn't work since he bolted."

"Constantin knows Matias is in town?" Quint asked.

"It surprised me, too, but Lola's worlds were colliding so she asked Constantin to give her a chance to work things out with Matias about Lili," Ree said.

"Did she say how long Matias has been in town?" Quint asked.

Ree shook her head. And then it dawned on her why he would ask in the first place. "That's the reason Constantin installed spyware on her computer, isn't it?"

"Jealousy can make a man do stupid things," Quint said. "Someone like Constantin wouldn't know what it is to trust another person's word."

Ree nodded agreement there. Boundaries and trust weren't exactly in the vernacular of most criminals. Those who'd made it to the top built their empires on power, greed and fear, using fear to breed loyalty.

"You already heard Lola is off tomorrow," Ree said.

"Are you guys planning to meet up for Pilates class in the morning?" he asked.

"No. I don't want to seem too eager to hang out," she said. "Angie has been great for forging a relationship with Lola. But classes every morning might make me seem too available. Plus, I need to personalize the apartment if we're going to have guests over again."

"And we are newlyweds. We wouldn't want to be away from each other too often," he pointed out.

"Exactly," she said as she looked around. "I have to say, we've moved up compared to the cabin."

"I would agree with you there," he said.

"Which also reminds me of Zoey," she said. "I wonder how she's doing in Austin."

"Better than she was in Cricket Creek, no doubt," he

said. "I can ask Grappell to check up on her while we're undercover if it would make you feel better."

"That would be great," she said.

"He can check on your grandfather as well," he continued.

"If he digs around in my personal life, he might not be well received," she reasoned. "As much as I want to confirm my grandfather is fine, I have to trust someone would have gotten word to me if anything had happened."

She also didn't need the distraction of thinking of home while on a case. Why the same logic didn't apply to Zoey was a puzzle, but it didn't, and Ree wanted to know how the young woman from their last case was doing. Ree had convinced the eighteen-year-old to go to a battered women's shelter when her no-good boyfriend was arrested. Zoey was a sweet young woman who needed a hand up to thrive. At least, Ree prayed Zoey hadn't checked herself out and gotten into trouble again. She really was a good person who'd landed in a bad situation.

Ree thought about the puppy she'd planned to foster to give Zoey something to look forward to when she was able to stand on her own two feet again.

"Everything okay?" Quint asked. She looked up at him only to realize he'd been studying her.

"Yes," she responded, shaking off her reaction to his concern. "Of course. It's just thinking about a sweet young person being manipulated by a boyfriend, or anyone for that matter, makes me sad."

"Thanks to you, Zoey is getting the help she needs,"

Quint said, and there was so much compassion in his voice.

She blinked a few times trying to stem hot tears that were threatening to flow, and focused on the rim of her wineglass.

"You should be smiling and celebrating," he said comfortingly, bringing his hand up to her chin before lifting it until her eyes met his. "Without you, that young woman would be out on the streets right now. I doubt she would have listened to reason. The fact that you cared about her showed her there are good people in the world who want the best for her. I seriously doubt she's ever experienced that kind of unconditional care in her life."

If she didn't want to cry before, she really had to work not to now. "Thank you, Quint. Thank you for saying those sweet words. They mean more to me than you could possibly know."

This time, she leaned forward and kissed him. Not for show. Not to sell the cover story. Not to convince someone the two of them were in love. But because she wanted to.

QUINT PULLED BACK from the kiss first, pressing his forehead to Ree's, thinking how easy it would be to get caught up in the moment, lost in her, and then what? Ruin a great working relationship? There hadn't been anyone since Tessa he wanted to be alone in a room with, let alone trusted enough to work beside.

His feelings for Ree were inconvenient. And they had to stop. She was emotional, seeking comfort. That was the only reason for the kiss. Period. His heart tried to mount a defense, but he couldn't lead with something he didn't trust. His heart had kept him from pushing Tessa to tell Bjorn about the pregnancy. Tessa had done such a great job of pleading and convincing him to go against his better judgment.

"It's her, isn't it?" Ree asked quietly. "You're thinking about her right now, aren't you?"

"How could you tell?" He truly wanted to know. He'd been a master at hiding his true feelings and making everyone believe he was all right. Not much got past Ree. She seemed to catch on every time he fell into the sinkhole that was thinking about Tessa and her baby.

"The way you get quiet. It's like someone sucked all the air from the room and you have to slow down so you can breathe again," she said. "Are you sure the two of you never dated?"

The question was the equivalent of a knife in the chest. It took a long moment for him to catch his breath and respond.

"If we had, I would have told you up front," he said, and he could hear the coldness creeping into his own voice. "I barely knew you before and had no reason to lie."

"It's just that you get so intense when you're thinking about her," she said quietly. "It stands to reason that your feelings might have gone deeper than you are willing to admit."

He shook his head.

"I know exactly where I stand on my and Tessa's friendship. We couldn't have been closer if we'd been

blood related. Others in the department couldn't believe
we weren't a couple, but I thought maybe you knew me
a little better than that by now," he said, stopping before he blurted out what he really wanted to tell Ree.
The truth was that he never felt toward Tessa the way
he felt every time he was around Ree. How was that
for messed up?

Ree pulled away from him and took a sip of her
wine. The air was cold where she'd been a few seconds
ago. He followed her lead and took a swig of beer, sitting back, rubbing the scruff on his chin.

"We need to come up with a plan to meet Constantin," he said, redirecting the conversation. They'd
talked about him enough for one night. He knew where
this was coming from. The past had been dredged up
ever since the phone call with Bjorn. Hell, he'd been
dealing with his frustration all day as a result.

Ree was observant, insightful. She would have read
him earlier and known exactly why he hated the idea
of cooperating with another agency. She deserved a lot
of credit for not calling him out on it or requesting he
remove himself from the case.

"I have an idea about that," Ree said. "But I'm guessing Lola will be in Galveston tomorrow with him, and
I'll be at work tomorrow night. Plus, she's met both
of us, so if we turn up in Galveston unexpectedly it'll
raise a red flag."

"Not a good idea, especially this early in the case,"
he said.

"Which is why I think we should set the alarm, grab
a couple hours of sleep and check up on his warehouse

operation. It would probably be best to follow up under the cover of night when it's too dark to recognize anyone," she said.

"True, but you have to get through a shift tomorrow night. Won't that be hard to do without enough sleep?" He didn't want to be the one to push her past a breaking point. As for Quint, he could get by on forty-five-minute naps throughout the day just fine. Most people weren't in the same boat.

"Since I'm not going downstairs to work out in the morning, I can sleep in," she said. "Didn't Agent Grappell give us an address nearby for the warehouse?"

"It's not too far, on the outskirts of the south side of the city," he said. "I can show you on the map if you'd like." He'd already mapped out the route from the docks in Galveston to the warehouses.

"I'll see it for myself in a few short hours." She shook her head. "I should probably get ready for bed and try to grab as much sleep as possible before we head out."

"What time should I set the alarm for?" he asked.

"How about four a.m.? That should give me time to brush my teeth and throw on a jogging suit," she said.

"Just shy of three hours away," he said, taking a sip of beer and settling into the sofa.

"This should help." Ree pushed up to standing and then drained her glass. She returned it to the kitchen before disappearing into the bathroom.

Quint grabbed the laptop and pulled up Google Maps. He plotted the most direct course to the warehouse. There would be no weapons out in the open.

Constantin was smarter than that. The legitimate shipping business had to operate as a front for his criminal activity. Who would really notice if a shipment disappeared off the books every once in a while? In a big shipping operation like this one, paperwork could "disappear," giving Constantin the opportunity to load up the occasional semi. A vehicle that large could carry an unimaginable amount of firepower. A shipment every few weeks or months could slip under the radar. The other possibility, of course, was breaking up a large shipment of weapons into smaller ones and loading them onto multiple trucks either with a false bottom or using a cargo net to hold cases underneath the trailer. In these cases, the required pit stops to check weight might be just a little off the manifest. Since scales weren't exact, a lot of illegal cargo and drugs made it across the US border using this method.

While he was online, he checked the case file to see if Driver had uploaded a report. There was nothing. So far, all he and Ree had been told about the other team was they were DEA, which meant drugs were involved. A shipping operation could move drugs in the ways Quint had already considered. The twist with narcotics of any kind was finding a way to throw off drug-sniffing dogs, difficult but not impossible. Getting away with illegal activity meant always staying one step ahead of law enforcement.

There were two facts that when put together didn't give the impression Driver was going to play fair on this case. First, the unannounced visit that could have put the whole investigation in jeopardy. Second, the lack of an update.

Quint's hands involuntarily fisted. He took in a couple of deep breaths in an attempt to calm down. As it was, he had an urge to find Driver and tell him what he thought about his secrecy and sterling record.

Driver wasn't the only reason Quint was frustrated tonight. He'd blown an opportunity to tell Ree how he really felt about her, to let her know how special she was to him. Little did she realize his friendship with Tessa was no threat to how he felt about Ree. He and Tessa had been more brother and sister than anything else, and that was exactly how they'd kept it. The kicker with Tessa came in the form of not being able to protect her, and in not being able to keep her baby safe.

Both *should* be alive. Tessa had been due last month. Tessa had been afraid she wouldn't get the "mom" gene. She'd feared the baby would grow up and hate her. Quint had calmly reassured Tessa none of those fears were going to come to fruition because she had him to help keep her on track as a parent. She wasn't alone in this. And the fact that she was this concerned before the baby was even born meant she was most likely going to be an amazing parent.

As far as Ree was concerned, he also realized anything beyond a working relationship would be out of the question. The quickest way to kill a good partnership was to date.

No matter how strong his feelings were or how much they seemed to grow as he got to know her, it was probably for the best for him to leave the topic alone.

Muddying the waters in their work relationship was the surest way to lose her. He couldn't take another hit like that.

"Your turn," Ree said as she exited the bathroom.

"I'm good," he responded.

"Okay, you'll wake me up in a couple of hours, then?" She stood at the doorway to the bathroom, looking like she was resisting the urge to speak up about whatever was on her mind. The way she looked at him convinced him the questionable subject was him.

"With a bucket of ice water," he said, smiling, trying to break up some of the sudden tension in the room.

"This seems like a good time to remind you that I sleep with my gun next to the bed," she teased back.

"Gentle shaking it is," he reassured. "And make sure the safety is on on that weapon."

"Always," she shot back before crossing over to the bed.

He refocused on the screen, ignoring the urge to join her.

Chapter Fourteen

Quint's whiskey-over-ice voice drew Ree out of a deep sleep.

"Time to wake up," he repeated quietly. There was nothing quiet about the reaction her body was having to him standing so close, whispering next to her.

She blinked her eyes open to a dimly lit room that cast shadows over his carved-from-granite jawline. The day-old stubble on his chin gave him an even more rugged look. *Sexier.* Ree sat straight up, pulling the covers to her chin.

"I'm good," she said, needing to put a little space between her and his unique spicy male scent. As she breathed in, he filled her senses. Her pulse kicked up a couple of notches, making caffeine a little less necessary. Turned out, all she needed was Quint standing next to her to wake her up.

"Coffee?" he asked.

"Are you actually an angel?" she teased, needing to redirect her thoughts to something lighter and less sexy than Quint Casey.

"On it," he said, walking away with a knowing smile.

Ree took in a deep breath and threw the covers off. She headed straight for the bathroom and splashed cold water on her face. After brushing her teeth, she pulled her hair off her face in a ponytail and dressed in an all-black jogging suit that should help her blend into the darkness.

She joined Quint in the kitchen.

"Here you go," he said, handing over a fresh brew.

"You are definitely an angel," she said with a smile.

"No one has ever accused me of being that before," he lobbed back. It was nice to see him in a lighter mood. After the phone call with Bjorn yesterday she was more than a little concerned he'd gone to a dark place that he wouldn't be able to return from.

She wiggled her eyebrows and took a sip of coffee after blowing on it. "How do you make the perfect pot every time?"

"I'd tell you, but I'd have to kill you." This time, he pretended to cut his own throat with his finger as a knife, and what should have looked corny turned out sexy instead. "Ready?"

"As much as I'll ever be," she said in response, noticing that he'd changed into a black T-shirt and jeans. Even his running shoes were a dark gray that would easily disappear in the darkness.

She secured her weapon in her bellyband holster and made sure her zip-up covered it. There shouldn't be any activity in the building at this late or early hour—depending on how one looked at it.

Quint opened the door for her, then followed her to the elevator. They made it down to the truck without running into a soul, as expected. The drive to the warehouse district took roughly forty minutes. The roads were narrow two-lane jobs. The streetlamps were few and far between. There was an abundance of fields on both sides of the road and weeds tall enough to touch Ree's backside if she got out of the truck here.

Remote locations were always eerie. There were generally only a couple of ways in or out. The moon was full, though, and that provided extra lighting. It was gorgeous, too.

"Everything okay over there?" Quint finally broke the silence.

"Ever just sit outside and look at the moon?" she asked, thinking it was probably an odd question for a person like Quint. He didn't strike her as the type to sit outside and marvel at nature.

"Would it surprise you to know that I have?" he asked.

"As a matter of fact, yes," she admitted.

"Why is that?" he continued.

"I just don't see you sitting around a campfire while looking up at the stars," she said.

"Not at my age, no," he said. "When my mother died, I was so angry that I didn't know what to do with myself or all that pent-up frustration. I took off running and didn't stop until my chest felt like it might burst. I realized I'd stopped at this huge lake. Eyes wet, chest heaving, I dropped down and lay on my back next to the water. When I looked up, the cloudless sky was an incredible shade of deep blue. There were so many stars it would take five lifetimes to count them all. The sky was like a crystal canopy over the earth. The full moon dialed up the brilliance. Ever since then, I make sure to get outside once a week and look up at the sky. Full moons like this one are my favorites."

"That's a beautiful story, Quint." Ree was without words as to how much it meant to her that he'd shared it.

"Let's hope the full moon tonight is our good-luck charm." He pulled the truck into the first lot.

"Where is All Transport?" she asked, looking at warehouses and lots that extended as far as the eye could see. There was very little lighting in each parking lot.

"Halfway down, there should be a street. All Transport should be three warehouses to the right," he informed her as he checked his cell phone.

"But you have a better idea than driving up or around the building, don't you?" she asked.

He nodded.

"I figured we could walk back here by the wire fencing and then cut a left through the buildings," he said. "Make our way over on foot. It'll be the quietest way to get over there and easier to get the lay of the land."

"Agreed."

"You're welcome to stay back here as an anchor or come with me." He held up an earpiece they could use to communicate back and forth with through a cell phone. "Or we can both go." His next option came with two earpieces and communication devices. "Your decision."

"Easy one," she said. "I'm coming."

"Okay. Then take the spare key in case we get separated or one of us needs to hightail it out of here," he said.

She pulled up their location on her cell phone. "The four-way stop we went through a couple of blocks ago is our rendezvous point." It would be their meetup if all hell broke loose, which happened in these scenarios. Ree had noticed it happened less often when she had a solid plan in place.

"Four-way stop it is," he said before checking the time. "It's almost five a.m., so, say, six fifteen?"

"Sounds good to me," she said. Should the situation get ugly, they needed to give the area time to settle down before trying to meet again. An hour should be plenty of time, but this was the worst-case-scenario plan. They were wired with comms devices and could literally stay in each other's ears as they split up.

Ree secured her comms device and earpiece. She tucked her cell phone underneath the seat and pocketed the key in a zipper pocket before exiting the truck. The current plan was to stick as close together as possible as Quint met her around the back of the vehicle. She let him take the lead since he'd been the one to study the area while she'd slept. She'd seen enough to get her bearings, marking notable landmarks as they made their way down the back alleyway near the fence.

The tall metal fence would almost certainly be wired. Three rows of barbed wire at the top gave this area a prison yard feel. The dome lights at the back of each warehouse provided a weirdly uniform look.

Three warehouses, then a left turn. There was enough space in between each building to maneuver a semi even though the bay doors were in front. Each building had one bay in back large enough to accommodate a semi. There was a metal door underneath the dome light. And a concrete block leading to the door. There were a few parking spots cordoned off with yellow stripes. The uniformity of it all gave more credibility to the prison look.

The concrete below her, on the other hand, was cracked and had potholes the size of her foot. She had to navigate carefully so as not to roll an ankle. An injury at this point would get in the way.

There was a dotting of vehicles parked behind the buildings. They had to stay close enough to a building and stay flat against it, should someone walk out of the building for a smoke break, but far enough away not to be picked up by the cameras. Those were predictable, too. Most of them pointed directly at the bay doors, which made the most sense. The biggest threat would be robbers.

Quint's hand came up, fisted. Ree froze.

QUINT HEARD A door open in the direction they were headed. He flattened his back against the wall, and Ree followed suit. A pair of male voices followed. He strained to hear the gist of their conversation.

"Mack is on his way for the drop-off. You can't be here," one of the men said. Based on his voice, it was impossible to get a sense of his size and weight.

"You keep talking about how great his stuff is, man," the second guy stated. "It's time you introduced me to this Mack person."

"No can do," guy one said. "Go the hell back inside before he gets here."

There was a long pause.

"All right. All right. Don't get your panties in a wad," the second male acquiesced.

The problem was, the sound of guy number one's footsteps meant he was coming around the side of the building in about three…two…one…

Quint reacted instinctively, reaching out for the guy and spinning him around until his back was against Quint's chest and Quint's right hand was over the guy's mouth, his left arm wrapped around the guy's thick torso. Thick Guy tried to bite Quint's hand as he threw an elbow backward, connecting with Quint's rib cage. Quint grunted as air expelled from his lungs. Thick Guy left Quint no choice.

He dropped his left hand, putting Thick Guy into a choke hold. The guy tried to shout, but couldn't get enough air in his lungs to make it happen. He tried to wriggle his way out of Quint's death grip. Also not going to happen. Not on Quint's watch.

Thick Guy tensed and jerked until the fight was drained from him. Then he went limp in Quint's arms before dropping onto the concrete.

"Help me position him," Quint whispered to Ree, a little winded himself after the altercation.

Ree came around and situated Thick Guy into an upright sitting position. She put his hands in his lap, his head to one side, and then crossed his legs before the two of them sprinted toward the target warehouses.

"We don't have a whole lot of time before the guy

back there comes to," Quint said to Ree. She'd linked their fingers as they ran, pushing the pace.

"I know," she responded. "Let's just get eyes on the location and drop off one of the devices you brought to see who comes by here and if we can ascertain whether or not this is where weapons are coming through."

He hadn't told her about the camera that was the size of a pin or the listening device that was the size of his thumbnail. He wouldn't need to for her to realize he'd brought them. The law said the devices couldn't be placed on private property. Public land was a whole different story, though. Sidewalks were fair game. The listening device had decent range. The sound could be amplified. But it needed to be within reasonable reach of the building to be able to pick anything up. Its success depended on whether or not there were any devices that might block it. If there were, Quint could be certain illegal activity occurred at this site. Gathering evidence in a defensible way in court was the issue.

Ree squeezed his hand as the buildings came into view. There was activity on this side of the warehouse district. Trucks moving in low gear and dimmed lights. He counted three from this distance. Two heading toward their target and one moving away. The low hum of the engine cut through the quiet night.

A vehicle with a loud motor roared from a short distance behind them. The drug dealer?

It took less than a minute for the sound of tires peeling rubber to split the air.

"Hey," a male voice called out.

Ree hit the deck, pulling Quint down with her. He

practically landed on top of her and didn't bother to shift his weight off her so as to provide cover. He balanced on his hands and feet, hovering over her instead of crushing her.

"Abort," he whispered, but she shook her head.

"Let's give it a minute," she said so low he could barely hear her.

"Bad idea," he said, unable to keep the dark-cloud feeling at bay.

Ree stayed silent as the commotion from behind them died down. It was far enough away that it didn't seem to rattle any cages over here. Maybe Ree was right and they could make a fast drop before hightailing it out of there. Quint had never been one to question his own decisions, and yet his instinct to abandon the mission had been wrong. He'd snapped to judgment when he should have stayed calm instead and analyzed the situation.

Not good, Casey.

He'd never questioned his ability to do his job effectively before now. Quint needed to have a sit-down with his partner when they got back to the apartment.

"Looks clear," she finally said. "Ready?"

He shook his head before rolling away from her. "You go."

Quint looked up at the full moon and the blanket of stars against a cobalt blue sky.

"Are you sure?" she asked, sounding a little confused.

"Positive." He rolled onto his stomach. "I'll stay

here and keep watch, provide cover if needed. You're smaller. It might be easier for you to get in and out."

"Okay," she said, not wasting a second or maybe just not giving him a minute to rethink the offer. Either way, she was off to the races. Quint pulled his gun from his holster and palmed it, ready to fire if need be. His thumb hovered over the safety mechanism, and his trigger finger was ready to tap should the need to protect Ree arise.

He watched her dark silhouette as she kept a low profile, moving across the parking lot with ease. She zigzagged back and forth to trees before crouching low, he guessed to drop a device. After moving to a second location in much the same manner, she made her way back. Trusting her had been the right move.

After holstering his weapon, he hopped up in one fluid motion and led them back toward the truck. Instead of going to the back fence, they made a wide circle, coming at the truck from the opposite side of the street. The second they cleared the last building and the truck came into view, Quint froze.

There were two guys circling his truck.

Chapter Fifteen

Ree tugged Quint's hand until he moved back a couple of steps. The doors of the truck were locked. The registration would trace back to a made-up name and address in North Texas. Her cell phone was tucked underneath the passenger seat, out of view. They hadn't left anything in plain sight that could tie them to law enforcement. The tackle box wasn't even inside the truck. There was nothing to panic about.

Except her heart raced and her pulse thumped at the base of her throat. The pair of idiots wore ripped sleeves. Nothing out of the ordinary for a warehouse district. In fact, they looked like truck drivers, but they could be dockworkers with those thick arms. It would also explain the lack of sleeves. No doubt these were friends of the guy who'd been stepping outside to meet his dealer.

From this distance, she couldn't hear their voices to know if one of the guys had tried to follow his co-worker outside. She didn't want to be any closer to them as they studied the truck. One took his cell phone out of his front pocket and snapped a couple of pictures.

One of the license plate. Even if this guy had a way to track the plate, which she highly doubted, it would lead to a dead end.

Metal glinted in the second guy's right hand. Ree realized what he was up to a moment before he bent down and sliced a tire. Well, that was going to be a headache to replace. Once the guys grew bored, she would retrieve her cell phone and any incidental items that could identify them, and they could abandon the truck.

The jerk with the knife tried to break the driver's-side window by slamming the butt of the knife into it. All he accomplished was drawing his hand back as the knife went flying. He moved toward it and shook his head before bending down and picking up the blade. Then he palmed the handle and jabbed the tip into all four tires.

Headlights cut through the darkness, sending the two jerks running back toward the warehouse where she and Quint had encountered the guy who'd been trying to score drugs. The semi drove on by as Quint leaned against the building. He exhaled. Slowly. He pinched the bridge of his nose like he was trying to stem a headache.

On a sigh, he said, "Ready?"

"As much as I'll ever be," she said.

They reached the vehicle and retrieved her cell and a backpack. Quint emptied the insurance papers from the dash, stuffing them inside the bag. He grabbed the license plates next. Those, too, went inside. He pocketed his burner phone as they emptied their communication devices along with earpieces in with the plates.

Quint zipped and shouldered the backpack before they headed back the way they'd come. On foot this time. Ree checked for bars and, thankfully, got a couple.

"We should be good to go as soon as we're clear of this place," she informed him.

He grunted in response.

By the time the sun came up, they'd walked within range to get an Uber. Quint made the call to Bjorn to arrange to have the truck towed and provide a replacement vehicle. It was long past breakfast when the Uber driver pulled up a block from their building, where they'd asked to be let out.

Ree could only imagine what they must look like. Hell? Or was that too kind a word? Her thighs burned from the morning's walk coupled with last night's shift. Her stomach growled because they'd both decided to go straight home rather than ask the driver to stop at a drive-through. But it was the humiliation burning her the most. How had they allowed those jerks to get to their vehicle?

"Are you ready for a light run?" Quint asked, clearly thinking the same thing she was. They could jog back to the building.

"Not really, but let's do it anyway," she said.

Quint laughed, and it was the first break in tension in what had turned into a monster of a morning. The quick trip to plant comms devices and maybe gather a little intel was successful in that they'd accomplished their mission. Having to abandon their vehicle and request a replacement was the worst.

Ree picked up the pace, jogging past Quint. Being competitive, he blew past with a laugh. He might be pretending not to be tired, but she heard the heavy breathing as he went by. Saving her energy, she was close enough to home to be able to pull off one last burst of energy as they rounded the corner to their building. Seeing the front doors, Ree turned up the gas. She pushed her legs and pumped her arms, barely passing Quint in time to smack her hand on the glass.

"I won," she said before pushing the door open and bolting toward the elevator.

The next thing she knew, he sprinted past her, reaching the elevator button a few seconds before she did.

"Who won now?" he quipped.

"Guess the first one to the apartment breaks the tie," she said, throwing a playful elbow into his ribs as she pushed past him into the elevator.

He gave a lot of side-eye when he joined her, but the corners of his lips upturned into a grin. As they neared the seventh floor, Ree realized he would be ready for her tricks this time. So she positioned herself in front of him to face him, grabbed two fistfuls of his black T-shirt and hauled him toward her. Pushing up to her tiptoes, she planted a steamy kiss on Quint's mouth.

For a moment, she got lost. The faint ding of the elevator registered, bringing her thoughts back to the present. She pulled on all her strength and shoved off, using his chest as leverage. He took a step backward, looking a little dazed as she pivoted and then raced to their door. Her flat palm smacked against it, and her body soon followed. Her left shoulder stopped the momentum, landing hard against the surface.

It caught her off guard that Quint didn't soon follow. She looked in time to see him launch himself toward the opening as the doors closed. Ree laughed. She couldn't help herself. The indestructible Agent Quinton Casey at a loss?

Pride filled her chest that she could knock him off balance at least half as much as he did her. She pulled the door key from her pocket and bolted inside as the elevator doors opened again and he shot toward her like a bullet.

"I win," she shrieked, unable to stop laughing.

"Because you cheated," he said, closing and locking the door behind him.

"Winning is winning," she said. "Besides, I didn't tell you to stand there once those doors opened. That was your choice."

He mumbled something she couldn't quite make out and probably didn't want to anyway. It couldn't have been good considering his tone. But then they both broke out laughing.

"You took this round, Sheppard. But the game is not over yet," he said.

"Really? Because I'm pretty sure the game ended when I tagged the front door first," she shot back.

"We'll see about that," he said as he walked right past her. He sat down at the counter and opened his laptop. His expression turned serious. "I'm pretty certain we're about to get dressed down by Bjorn for losing the truck."

"These things happen," she said, taking the chair next to him. "Plus, we took all the necessary precautions. We couldn't have anticipated a drug deal at nearly five o'clock in the morning."

"Murphy's Law," he agreed.

"It could have been worse. We're both still here," she said without thinking. Damn. Damn. Damn. If she could reel those words back in, she would. "Sorry, Quint." She reached over and touched his arm. His muscles tensed with contact. She apologized again and withdrew her hands.

"Promise me something," Quint said, and his voice became serious enough to make the hairs on the back of her neck prick.

"No can do until I hear what you're asking," she said, sitting up a little straighter and folding her arms across her chest.

"Give me your word you won't go behind my back to Bjorn at any time during this investigation." He didn't look up or over when he said the words that were equivalent to daggers in the heart.

"I can't make that promise, and you never should have asked," Ree stated flat out. This apartment suddenly felt too small. With nowhere else to go to get a little breathing room from Quint, she marched into the bathroom, making it just in time for the first tear to spring from her eyes.

AN EMAIL UPDATE came in from Agent Grappell. It was about Zoey. Quint read it and immediately jumped up from the stool. He made a beeline for the bathroom door. His first thought was how relieved Ree would be when she heard the news. He raised his fist to knock, then froze midreach.

In his estimation, he was the last person she wanted to see, let alone speak to. Damn. He needed to get outside and get some air. Ree's cell phone buzzed as he walked by it on the counter. He kept going until he was out of the apartment, out of the elevator and out of the building.

Maybe he could walk off his frustration at the very least.

Forty minutes later, and Quint was no closer to an answer as to why he'd felt the need to ask Ree not to go to Bjorn. She balked because he'd been a jerk. An apology didn't seem nearly enough to undo the damage. She had every right to be frustrated with him. Hell, he was angry with himself.

A few more blocks and he'd turn back. The least he could do while he was out here was refocus on the case. There could be another update from Agent Grappell by now. Quint had blown out of the apartment in such a hurry he'd left his cell phone behind. But he never went anywhere without a weapon. His was secured in the ankle holster strapped underneath his pants leg.

By now, Ree should be out of the bathroom. She deserved to know what was going on with Zoey, so he started the trek back, picking up speed the closer he got to the building. As he rounded the corner, he almost slammed into a guy. Quint sidestepped in the nick of time, but a voice in the back of his mind told him to halt. The guy he'd almost slammed into was Nick Driver.

Quint spun around. "Hold on there."

Driver stopped but didn't turn, so Quint walked directly over to the man. "You live in my building, don't you?" Quint said, staring him in the face.

Driver nodded, looking a little less than comfortable around Quint. Good. Driver *should* be cautious.

"Then maybe you've heard about me by now?" Quint continued, undaunted.

"I have," Driver stated, his lips compressed like he was holding his tongue. *Good.*

"This case will go a whole lot easier if we both make an attempt to get along. Don't you agree?" Quint said, holding back as much of his frustration as he could.

"I was just about to suggest the same," Driver said, trying a little too hard to mask the fear in his voice by coming off overly confident.

"Then from here on out we work together, right?" Quint asked.

Grudgingly, Driver nodded again. A muscle in his jaw ticked, but he didn't seem stupid enough to challenge Quint. Since there was no use in standing there in the morning heat, he said goodbye and walked past Driver.

Quint passed Angie on the street as he headed toward the front doors. He hoped she hadn't heard what had just gone down.

"Morning," she practically chirped.

"How's the studying going today?" he asked with a courtesy smile.

"About to get started." She held up a thick workbook. "Heading out to a coffee shop so I won't get distracted by cleaning the apartment."

"If you don't pass the test, you could always use that thing as a weapon," he quipped, motioning toward her workbook, trying to keep the mood light.

Angie laughed.

"I guess it could do some damage if needed." She shook the book. "Yep. Definitely."

"Keep it close by," he continued. "Just in case."

"Did you go for a run?" she asked.

"Guilty," he said. "But I wouldn't call it much of a run."

"Take it easy," she said. "Or Ree will kick your rear end."

"She does all the time," he joked before exchanging goodbyes.

The elevator seemed to be taking its sweet time once he got inside. He made it up to seven, selfishly hoping Ree would still be awake. In case she'd dozed off, he slipped inside quietly.

"I'm home," he whispered, not wanting to surprise someone who carried a weapon at all times.

"I'm awake," she said. The reassurance was appreciated. "Where did you take off to?"

"Went for a walk while you showered," he said. "Tried to clear my head."

"Did it work?" she asked. The tension in her voice said he'd lost ground with her.

"Probably not." He joined her at the counter. "When did you get out of the bathroom?"

"A minute ago," she said.

"Good. I wanted to be the first to tell you that we received an update on Zoey while you were in there," he said. "She's still at the women's shelter in Austin and, according to one of her counselors, is making real progress."

Ree exhaled, and her chest deflated. A look of pure relief washed over her features.

"That's the best thing I've heard all day," she said with a lightness in her tone that had been missing earlier.

"I should probably let you know that I ran into Driver on my way back to the building," he stated.

"Oh?" she asked as an eyebrow arched. "How did that go?"

"Good. I think," he said. "He seems clear on where I stand with him. That's always a good thing, right?"

"Depends," she said on a sigh. "On whether that makes him easier or harder for me to work with now."

"I'm going out on a limb here, but I'll say easier," he said.

The small shift in her caused his chest to puff out, and all he could think about was the steamy kiss in the elevator earlier.

He walked away before he did anything to rekindle that fire.

Chapter Sixteen

The news about Zoey perked up Ree's spirits. "What about the truck?"

"Bjorn responded to my email. She's handling it," Quint stated with a frown.

"That doesn't sound good," Ree said. "What did she say?"

"Probably not words I should repeat," he said. "Something about hell freezing over before we get a new vehicle. She's having the truck towed and new tires put on. She said the fastest she can get it back to us is tomorrow and that we'd just have to walk until then if we needed to get somewhere."

"Ouch." She stretched, thinking she should probably rest a little while before her shift tonight. At least it was Tuesday and wouldn't be crowded at the bar. "It's probably too early to pick up anything on surveillance. I dropped the camera in a good spot. Not sure I was able to get close enough for the listening device."

"You did what you could considering how everything went down," he said.

"If we keep the same truck, it'll be hard to go back to the warehouses," she reasoned.

Quint nodded.

"Too bad Lola isn't working tonight." Ree figured she'd made inroads with Lola and wanted to capitalize on the progress. "Any word about Esteban or Matias?"

"Hold on, I'll check." Quint refocused his attention on the laptop, turning the screen so they both could see. He checked his email first. There was nothing there from Grappell.

His cell buzzed before he could check the case file. He located it and checked the screen, sucking in a breath when he saw the number. "Hello."

There was a moment of silence. Followed by him asking if he could put the call on speaker. The answer must've come quick because he glanced at Ree and gave a small headshake before standing up and moving back to the window he'd stared out during the last call with their boss. Ree had seen the number and knew exactly who was calling.

"I didn't…" He paused. "No." Another beat passed. "If he hadn't have…then I wouldn't have needed to."

From the sounds of it, Quint was being dressed down by the boss.

He said a few "Yes, ma'ams" into the receiver before ending the call.

"I'm betting that call had to do with your run-in with Driver a little while ago," she said, venturing a guess.

Quint issued another sharp sigh. "Apparently she got a call from Richard Magee."

"Because you had words with Nick Driver?" Communication from the head of the DEA seemed like over-kill. "Didn't you say that happened less than half an hour ago?"

He nodded. His lips thinned, and his gaze narrowed. Anger came off him in palpable waves.

"Hold on a second," she said. "This can't be right. Why would Magee get involved in a case this low down the line?"

"Turns out Driver and Magee are in-laws," he informed. "Driver married the guy's daughter."

"Nepotism?" she asked, but the question was rhetorical. "No wonder the man has so many accolades in his employment jacket."

"No one wants to upset the head honcho," Quint said with disgust. "There's probably some truth to his abilities in the field."

"I'm still good with taking communication lead with the other team. This doesn't change anything for me," she admitted. Her record might not have as many honors in it but she was confident in her abilities and her job as a top-notch agent.

"You might want to rethink being associated with me," he said, but she could see that he was just frustrated. An agent of Quint's caliber would take nepotism about as well as a sucker punch. In a fair fight, Quint would come out on top. Pull strings and he could end up in trouble. Any one of them could. One thing was certain. Their instincts about the DEA agent being trouble seemed spot-on.

"I'm good, Quint," she reassured.

He caught her gaze and held it for a long moment

before giving an almost imperceptible nod. "Let's get on with the case, then."

"Good. Where were we?" She picked up on a hint of appreciation and respect in his voice that made her swell with pride. Quint was a well-respected agent, and his opinion of her mattered. His respect was important to her, and his confidence in her gave her a boost.

Ree's cell buzzed. She picked it up and checked the screen.

"Looks like our counterparts are calling now," she said.

"What can I do for you?" she asked after exchanging pleasantries.

"I'm working with Agent Driver on the DEA side of the case, and I just wanted to call to apologize if my partner came across in the wrong way before," the agent said.

"Thank you, Agent—"

"Please, call me Shelly."

"Thanks for reaching out, Shelly. I believe our partners spoke earlier and cleared up any confusion between us," Ree stated.

"I'll do what I can on my end. My partner leans on his family ties a little too closely for my liking," the agent continued. "I hope this conversation stays between us."

"I have no reason to share," Ree said. The frustration in Shelly's tone sounded very real, and she was certainly saying all the right things. What legitimate agent would want to work with someone who was aided based on a family connection?

"I can share that we were brought on to this case as part of a bigger investigation into Matias Gimenez," the agent said.

"Gimenez is a drug runner?" Ree asked.

"Afraid so," Shelly confirmed. "We've been following him in Argentina, but he keeps coming back to the States. We didn't know he was heading to Houston until very recently."

"Because of his daughter, Lili," Ree said.

"That's correct. Gimenez works for a high-value target in Latin America," the agent continued.

"So he's powerful," Ree stated, thinking that if he got Lili back to Argentina, he had a chance of keeping her there and away from Lola.

"Very," Shelly said, then came, "Hold on."

The call became very quiet for a few long seconds.

"My partner is coming back and he isn't up-to-date on this call," Shelly said. "I have to go now, but I hope we can all work together."

"Wouldn't have it any other way," Ree stated.

The call ended.

Ree turned to Quint. "Well, that was an interesting conversation."

"I PIECED TOGETHER that Matias is the reason the DEA is involved," Quint stated, figuring the betrayal might have been the best thing that could have happened if it gave them an in with Shelly.

"He's powerful, Quint. If he takes Lili back to South America, Lola might never see her daughter again." Ree exhaled, and her shoulders rounded forward.

"We have to figure out a way to protect Lola and her daughter," he said without much internal debate. From what he could tell so far, Lola was a decent person who'd gotten wrapped up in a bad situation. He'd noted the phenomenon of intelligent women allowing men who were bad for them to slip past their radars. It happened more than it should, and he reasoned the men were usually charming, a common personality trait among narcissists. They could slide right in and break past normally guarded walls. He'd watched it firsthand with Tessa, who didn't put up with a whole lot of nonsense. Her baby's father had slithered around her carefully constructed walls, and Tessa had beaten herself up over allowing it.

"I'd like that very much," Ree stated. She paused a moment before shifting gears back to the agent and her phone call. "She didn't give me the impression she was thrilled to be working with Driver. I didn't have to read between the lines to pick up on it."

Quint nodded. "It hadn't occurred to me how awful it must be to get stuck on an assignment with him."

"It seems to be part of the reason she reached out to me," Ree said.

"When the call ended, I noticed you didn't say goodbye. In fact, your forehead wrinkled like it does when you're confused about something." He probably shouldn't have just admitted how well he knew her habits, but there it was.

A hint of pink colored her cheeks as she nodded. "She had to go because he was coming back. She didn't say from where, and she ended the call abruptly."

"You think we can trust her." It wasn't a question.

"Yes," Ree said, answering anyway.

"I agree," he said. "Reaching out to you put her at risk. She took all the chance in that exchange. She also gave you information we didn't have before and isn't showing up in the report."

"I'm guessing that was her way of extending an olive branch," Ree stated. "I just hope she's given due credit when this is all said and done. I have a feeling she'll be the one who deserves it between the two of them."

Quint nodded.

"Did Bjorn come down pretty hard on you?" she asked, wincing a little bit.

"Nothing I can't handle," he said, which was true. He didn't know how it might affect the case, and that bothered him. Could he have handed the DEA a reason to keep their cards close to their chests? Driver was already.

Quint's cell dinged. It was the sound attached to email notifications.

"Let's hope for some more good news," he said, moving to his laptop. The news about Matias sat in the back of Quint's mind as he powered up the device and then opened his email. Ree joined him.

"What does it say?" she asked, her back toward the kitchen.

"There's no record of Esteban entering this country legally, according to Agent Grappell," he informed.

"Which doesn't necessarily mean he's doing something illegal or came here to commit a crime," she pointed out.

"No, it doesn't. He could be here to support his sister," Quint reasoned. He'd been an only child, but Ree, on the other hand, came from a large family. As much as she'd talked about her brothers smothering her at times growing up, she'd also made it clear any one of them would walk through fire to save another. Was it the reason Esteban was in the country? To protect his sister in some way? Or his niece? The last thought resonated with Quint. Even though he'd never met Tessa's baby, he would have gone to any length to protect her after learning about the pregnancy. He'd felt an instant bond with the child, born out of his brotherly love for the baby's mother.

"Esteban is most likely here because of Lola and Lili," he said. "I can't prove it. Yet. But I'd bet my life savings on it."

Ree sat for a long moment before finally nodding in agreement.

"It makes sense when I really think about it," she said. "If I was a single mother, my brothers would want to protect me."

"Doesn't rule out criminal activity, though," Quint continued. "We don't know how he makes his living while he's in the States. Whatever he's doing, he must be getting paid under the table, because there's no IRS record of a salary."

"The IRS is the first place Grappell would look for employment records," Ree agreed.

"There's no Social Security record, either," he said before looking at her. "See if you can find out from Lola why they relocated to the US a few years ago."

"I can already tell you it coincides with having the baby," she said.

"Interesting," he noted.

"Isn't it?" she responded. Then added, "I haven't gotten Lola to talk about what brought her here, or met her brother, but I'm guessing it has to do with having the baby and not wanting her brought up in Argentina."

"Have you been there?" he asked.

"No." She shook her head. "Why?"

"Beautiful country in many respects. Beautiful people, too," he said. "Still a little too machismo for my taste, if you know what I mean."

"I can't imagine Constantin would be thrilled to know Lola's ex was in the country," Ree pointed out.

"I can't imagine it would go down well between the two of them," he agreed.

"Matias would get custody even if he wasn't tied to a powerful person." She caught on fast. Her sharp mind was one of her many incredible qualities.

"Unless she had connections, which I'm doubting in this situation," he said.

"Is there any chance Matias is the one who put the spyware on her computer?" Ree asked.

"Good question." He stopped to think about it. Would Lola ever allow Matias to be alone in the room with any of her personal items? He highly doubted it. "My first thought is no. Maybe you can get close enough to her to find out."

"She is still a puzzle to me," Ree said on a sigh. "I just keep going back to the fact that she doesn't give me any vibe that she would be involved in criminal activity."

"And yet it seems to be all around her," he pointed out. "We already mentioned the whole *birds of a feather flock together* saying. There's a certain amount of corruption in every country, and South America is no exception. She's either part of it or running from it."

"That's what I keep coming back to," Ree stated. "If she wasn't part of it, why does she seem to be surrounded by it all the time?"

Quint compressed his lips in a frown. *Birds of a feather?*

Chapter Seventeen

Ree had tried to rest after her conversation with Quint in order to be ready for her shift. Her mind kept churning over the new information instead. She dressed, ate a quick dinner salad with Quint, and was out the door and to work fifteen minutes early for her shift.

Lola was correct. Tuesdays were slow. There wasn't a whole lot to learn about being a barback. She worked for Annie, who was a popular bartender, but one who kept to herself on breaks. Glasses needed to be clean and at the ready at all times for the bar area Ree was responsible for. Garnishes needed to be chopped and ready to go. Basically, it was her job to make sure her bartenders had everything they needed, when they needed it. HNC didn't like its selective clientele standing around waiting for a drink a second longer than necessary.

Not having a whole lot to keep her busy made time tick by at the slowest possible pace. Midnight couldn't get there fast enough. Not five minutes after, Ree walked out the front door to a waiting partner.

"How was it?" he asked when he got a good look at her face.

"Don't ask," she responded, linking their arms as they walked the couple of blocks back to the apartment.

"Hungry?" he asked after they got through the door.

"Very." She toed off her shoes and loosened her bow tie. "Just let me change into something more comfortable."

He nodded before ducking into the kitchen as she made a beeline for the bathroom. Her robe hung on the back of the door, so she slipped out of her clothes and into the thick terry cloth. She secured the tie around her waist before joining him at the counter. "What is this amazing smell?"

"The best Tex-Mex restaurant in Houston if you can believe a 'rate my food' app." He nudged a plate of the best-looking enchiladas toward her.

"Sour cream chicken?" she asked, taking a deep breath and inhaling the scent of great food.

"For you," he said, "and a beef chimichanga for me."

Ree wasted no time eating her food. "I can't imagine better Tex-Mex than that."

"I forgot to get the drinks," he said.

"Who could care about drinks with food this amazing?" she teased.

He brought over a Coke for her and black coffee for himself.

"Excellent choices," she said.

"I aim to please," he said before asking if she learned anything tonight.

"Nothing new and very little in the way of tips. Note

to self, ask off Tuesdays," she said with a snort. "Did we get anything from our surveillance equipment?"

"The sound is terrible," he said, referring to last night's adventure. "We won't get anything useful from the listening device."

"Not a complete surprise," she said. "I couldn't really get close enough."

"The lab might be able to do more with it," he said. "Maybe not a total loss there."

"And the camera?" she asked, hoping the truck tires weren't slashed for no reason. The whole incident did get them in hot water with Bjorn.

"That one is better." His fingers flew across the keyboard as he pulled up footage. "The agents in Analysis will watch round the clock so we don't have to, but I did manage to record suspicious activity."

A pair of men walked to the opposite side of the truck in the middle of the day, making seeing what they were exchanging impossible. But they were trading something.

"Drugs?" she asked, figuring the warehouse district was a good place for narcotic sales. It was on the outskirts of town, and most of the business running out of there seemed legit.

"Could be," he said. "But watch as this guy walks around."

The camera homed in on a face.

"Esteban?" she asked.

"Looks like Lola, doesn't he?" he asked.

"It's a little grainy when it's blown up, but I can see

the resemblance," she said. "Does that mean he works for Constantin?"

"It could explain being paid under the table," he stated.

She nodded. A piece of her wished Lola weren't involved with sketchy people, but signs pointed elsewhere.

"I can't get over the fact that someone like Lola would attach herself to a guy dealing drugs in her homeland and then come here and get mixed up with someone who ran weapons," Ree said, thinking out loud.

"You like her, don't you?" he asked.

"Yes," she admitted. "But how could both of our intuitions about her be wrong? Gut instinct accounts for some, but we have training and experience to back it up."

"Have you ever been wrong? Misjudged someone?" he asked. "Because I have."

"You're right," she reasoned, trying to quash the niggling feeling struggling to convince her otherwise. "I've made a few mistakes."

"The really good ones can trick even a seasoned agent," he said. "Not a whole lot gets past my radar, and that used to make me cocky."

"What happened to change your mind?" she asked. He was right. She'd learned never to trust her instincts and to follow the evidence, but there was something about Lola—an innocence?—that had Ree second-guessing herself. The evidence so far pointed to Lola knowing exactly what she was getting into.

"There was a case in Dallas where I was one hundred percent certain a kid was innocent. He played the victim role with an abusive stepdad. His mother was a drunk and used to pass out at like eight o'clock every night on the couch. The stepdad was a class A jerk, doing everything from laundering money to running bootleg," he said. "Looking back, evidence pointed to the kid being involved. But I made excuses for that kid every step of the way. I bought the story that he was seventeen and stuck in a bad situation. Turned out he just looked young. He wasn't related to the woman passing out on the couch every night. Her son lived with his father in Oklahoma. This guy altered the kid's ID and was living on-site helping run the small-time business."

Ree wrinkled her nose. "Stinks to be wrong."

"Stinks to high heaven," he retorted. "The thing is, I kept catching him in lies but chalked it up to the abuse. There were no physical altercations. The guy was getting into bar fights and coming back cut up. The so-called stepdad had no idea this guy was telling on him, and I swore to my boss this kid wasn't involved and needed counseling services and a safe place to live."

"Why do you think he fooled you?" she asked.

"He came up with a story that had a few parallels to my own background. I guess I saw myself in that kid." He shrugged. "Some people are just evil manipulators."

"How did you figure it all out?" Ree asked, figuring every agent had a story about being snowed when they should know better.

"The real kid showed up to check on his mother when she didn't respond to his texts for a couple of days. He got worried and had his real father drive him down from Oklahoma to see if she was okay," he said. "We got her to sober up for a bit, and she cried pretty much nonstop. She was clueless about what was going on under her own roof because they plied her with alcohol every night and made sure she was passed out by a certain time. She had no idea one of the people under her roof was using her son's identity."

"Those are terrible people, taking advantage of someone with a disease like that," she said with disdain.

"There has to be a special place in hell for folks like them," he stated with enough heat to melt an ice cube in the dead of winter in Siberia.

"Agreed. And in our line of work, we get to be the ones to make sure they're locked up until they get there," she said. It was the main perk and something she needed to remind herself of almost daily, especially during a case. It could be a little too easy to focus on the bad side of their line of work and lose sight of the whole reason they did it.

Quint nodded.

"Did you ever follow up to find out what happened with the mom and son?" she asked.

"She got clean and stayed sober," he said. "Last I checked, which was almost a decade ago, she'd moved to Oklahoma to be closer to her son."

"That's a sweet ending," she said as warmth filled her. She also noted that the mistake he brought up was from more than a decade ago. "Quick question."

"Shoot," he said.

"Are you telling me you haven't pegged someone

wrong in more than ten years?" she asked, figuring there was no way.

"A hair more than fourteen to be exact," he said. "But Lola could prove me wrong on that point at any time."

Ree hoped she wouldn't.

QUINT CLEANED UP the dishes, figuring Ree needed to get sleep after last night and then working a shift. "Speaking of Lola, does she work Wednesdays?"

"I think so," Ree said. "I'm pretty sure I saw her name on the schedule."

"Good. I should probably figure out the vehicle situation so I can head down to Galveston tomorrow night while you're working and see what I can dig up on Constantin and his brother. There's a restaurant down the street from their place that I hope to dig around in," he said.

"Wish I could be there with you instead of at the bar," Ree said, sounding like a kid who'd just been told the candy ran out.

"You'll be busy with Lola, getting information," he said.

"That's the hope," she stated, rubbing the soles of her feet. He shifted his gaze away from the terry cloth robe and how it parted just above her knee, revealing the silky skin of her thigh. She pushed up to standing. "I'll grab a shower and hit the sheets."

He didn't want to think about how nice it would feel to be in bed beside her, or how easy it would be to get used to waking up next to her.

"I'll clean up in here and upload a report to the shared folder. The other couple in the building needs to know we've already been to Constantin's warehouse and that we've dropped comms devices. The analysts will share any data relevant to their case," he said, deciding he needed to refocus on something besides bed and Ree.

"Thank you," she said, "for taking care of all these details and, again, for keeping the good food rolling. I don't ever want to be on an assignment with anyone else but you. I'm used to fast-food tacos and burgers with maybe an occasional shake thrown in. You keep me fed with the most amazing food and even remembered my favorite drink is Coke."

"Don't worry about it," he said. "Besides, I'd throw on that uniform in a heartbeat and work as a barback if I could."

Ree laughed out loud, and it was the most musical sound. She really seemed to have no idea the effect she had on men, or more specifically on him. The last part was for the best, because there was no way a relationship between the two of them could go anywhere, he thought as she disappeared into the bathroom. He wasn't thinking right if he was even considering the consequences the two of them dating might have.

On a sharp sigh, he loaded the dishwasher and uploaded the info to the shared folder before closing down his laptop. Both of them could use a good night of sleep. He'd mapped out his Galveston trip earlier while Ree was at work, so there wasn't much more that could be done tonight anyway. It was a shame that she couldn't go with him, but the two of them together would be more easily recognizable now that Constantin had seen them when he'd picked Lola up from work. Going alone, Quint could throw on a ball cap and keep most of his face hidden.

By the time he shut everything down, Ree was out of the bathroom. He expected her to be asleep when he finished his turn. Instead, she was sitting on the bed under the covers, staring.

"Everything okay?" he asked as he climbed in bed.

"Yes, I'm just taking a few minutes to process," she said, patting her side of the bed.

He met her in the middle and she leaned into him, resting her head on his shoulder after he looped his arm around her shoulders.

"Do you ever think about leaving all this behind and having a family someday?" she asked. The question came out of left field.

"To be honest, not before Tessa was killed. I thought having a family was the worst thing a parent could do to a kid," he said.

"You do realize what you just said there," she said.

"I'm mostly referring to my father," he pointed out. "I've already told you my mother should have been nominated for sainthood."

"I don't even have time for a puppy," she said in a sleepy voice that tugged at his heartstrings.

"No. Not with a job like ours," he said.

"Have you ever considered how awful that is?" she asked.

"Not really," he admitted, thinking she was sleep-deprived and probably barely awake at this point. "I wouldn't mind getting a dog someday, but now is definitely not the right time."

"I don't even have time to foster a puppy for Zoey," she said, and now her words were a little slurred. She was definitely only barely awake.

"Not right now, you don't," he said. "But things could change."

"What things?" she asked. "Did you know that I'm thirty-six years old and still not married?"

"You don't look your age, and I mean that as a compliment," he stated before she could get defensive.

Ree yawned.

"I should have a puppy someday," she said.

"Yes, you should," he agreed, figuring she wouldn't remember this conversation in the morning.

"Do you want to have a puppy together?" she asked. "We could take turns taking care of it."

"That would make it hard to work on cases together, wouldn't it?" he asked, thinking how much he would hate to lose her as a partner even if that meant raising a puppy together.

"You would make beautiful puppies," she said through another yawn.

Quint couldn't help but laugh at that one.

"What did I say?" she asked.

"Nothing you'll remember in the morning," he said.

"We would have beautiful children," she said, curling up against his side.

Quint froze. For a split second, he could envision

their child. He'd want a little girl who looked exactly like her mother. Fatherhood? He shook off the reverie, thinking he would never be that cruel to a kid.

Chapter Eighteen

"I don't think I've slept so deeply in my entire life." Ree sat up and stretched her arms out with a yawn. The smell of fresh-brewed coffee wafted across the room, but there was no sign of Quint. "Hello?"

Panic settled over her for reasons she couldn't explain. He should be here. She threw off the covers and shuffled into the kitchen. Quint was gone. The bathroom door was open when she walked by, so she already knew he wasn't in there. She searched around for a note before locating her cell phone. There was no text or phone call.

Just as she was about to hit DEFCON 3, a key slipped inside the lock and the door handle jiggled. She moved to the door as it opened.

"Where did you go?" she asked, examining him for signs of injury. None were visible. He did, however, have a bagful of bagels from the café down the road. The fact that she'd overreacted caused her cheeks to flush.

"Bjorn arranged for a new truck to arrive overnight, so I inspected it. Looks almost as good as new," he said with a look of surprise stamping his features. He held up the bag. "While I was out, I decided to pick up breakfast."

Ree issued a sharp sigh.

"All good?" he asked with a raised eyebrow as he moved into the kitchen and set the bag on the counter.

"Yes. Sure. I guess." She walked around to the stool on the other side of the counter and sat down. "I'm confused about why I just had a massive reaction to my partner being gone in the morning on a bagel run." She put her head in her hands. "I slept so deeply and then woke in a panic when I realized you were gone."

"I'm here," he reassured her in that whiskey-over-ice voice of his. She reminded herself not to get too used to it. This case would end, and they would go back to their respective lives. There was no guarantee they would ever work together again.

"The odd thing is that we're nowhere close to wrapping up this case. Why would I panic if you weren't here?" If she couldn't figure it out, there was no way he would.

"It's probably just stress-related," he said. "No big deal."

"You're probably right," she said, hoping it was true.

"It'll pass," he said. "But I'm honored you would worry so much about my safety."

"You're important to me, Quint. Of course I'd be concerned about what happens to you," she stated as he passed a cup of coffee over.

"This should help," he said.

"You know what it is?" she asked after thanking him

and taking the offering. "I have a bad feeling about you going to Galveston alone tonight."

That had to be the problem. It was the only thing that made sense.

"I'll be careful," he reassured.

"I know," she said. "Just take a few extra precautions if you don't mind."

Women's intuition could be a powerful thing, and hers was issuing a warning. She figured it had to do with Quint.

"Should we let Shelly know about your trip tonight?" she asked.

"Nah, I'm only going to gather intel," he stated. "There's nothing to report yet."

She nodded, taking a sip of fresh brew, desperately needing the caffeine boost.

"You asked if I wanted to share a puppy last night," he said, handing over a plate of bagels and cream cheese.

"Oh, really?" she asked. "Was I awake?"

"You sounded out of it," he said. "How'd you sleep?"

"Great. Better than ever actually," she admitted. The feeling came back, but she ignored it. Quint was probably right. It was probably stress-related. She'd gone from one case to the next without enough time off in between, and then there was her grandfather. He was probably fine, too. She was on edge, blowing this whole morning out of proportion. "Normally, after a night of sleep like the one I just had, I'm refreshed in the morning."

"Maybe you need a few more nights of sleep to fully recover," he said.

"I guess so," she said. "It's odd."

"We're all off our game every once in a while," he said, holding a bagel plate of his own along with a fresh cup of coffee. "Should we log on and see if there are any updates this morning?"

"Why not?" she asked on a sigh, resigned to her strange mood. This wasn't good. Ree was never off her game while on a case. "I don't have to be at work for hours anyway."

Before Quint logged on, he retrieved her personal phone from the tackle box and held it out. "You'll feel a whole lot better if you check on your grandfather."

Ree took the offering with a smile.

"Thank you," she said before texting her brother Shane.

The response came back almost immediately.

He's good. Tired. But good.

Relief washed over her as she showed the screen to Quint.

"Looks like I was worried for nothing," she said.

"It shows how much you care and that's never for nothing," he countered before returning her cell to the tackle box, locking up and sitting next to her.

"Oh, look at this. We have an update from the other team." He clicked on a folder in the joint case file after logging on.

"Anything good in there?" she asked.

He skimmed the contents.

"Nothing we don't already know," he stated.

"Let me guess, Wonder Boy gave the update," she said.

"Looks like it," he confirmed.

"Well then, it has no chance of actually being useful," she said.

Quint laughed.

"You're in a mood this morning," he noted.

"Yes. Sorry. I don't know what's wrong with me," she admitted.

"Take it easy today, then," he said. "Rome wasn't built in a day, and this case won't live or die based on whether or not you take the morning off."

She polished off her bagel.

"I'm climbing back in bed, then," she said after brushing her teeth. She retrieved her coffee mug. "You can join me if you want." She quickly added, "To drink coffee and possibly go back to sleep."

"Shame," he said, low and under his breath, as he brought his laptop over. When he spoke again, he turned up the volume. "We can check the footage together."

"Or we could talk about something besides work for a change," she said, then realized how that sounded. "I mean, get to know each other a little better. We are supposed to be married, and although we did already work a case together, I think it was solved in record time."

"You want to talk?" he asked, but it was a rhetorical question. "We'll talk. Fair warning, though. I'm not all that good with words."

"I'll be the judge of that," she said with a smile. She was still puzzled by her reaction this morning and wanted nothing more than to put that behind her and start the day all over again.

On the bed with a topped-off cup of coffee, she positioned her pillows as a backrest. Quint moved beside her, sitting on top of the covers.

"Are you comfortable?" she asked.

He nodded and mumbled that he was as he opened the laptop. "How about you?"

"How about me what?" she asked, feeling the moment the air in the room shifted, charging with electricity.

"Comfortable?" he asked, and his voice had a sexy, husky quality to it.

"Yes" was all she could manage in response. The word came out as more of a croak than anything else. As it was, her throat dried up and her tongue felt like she'd licked a glue stick. She swallowed to ease the dryness, to no avail. She coughed to clear her throat. "Anything on the footage?"

He was pulling it up as she asked. "We'll know in a few minutes."

As he scrolled, she felt the warmth of his body against hers and the desire that flowered inside her. The kisses they'd shared suddenly took center stage in her thoughts as warmth flooded her. She couldn't help but wonder if Quint felt any of these same sensations, because she was suddenly the Fourth of July inside.

He shifted positions and studied the screen like it

was a bomb about to detonate and the only way to stop
it was with eye contact.

"Ree," he finally said.

"Yes," she answered.

"I'd very much like to kiss you right now," he said.

"What's stopping you?" she asked as a dozen butter-
flies released in her chest. Her stomach free-fell at the
prospect of their mouths fusing again.

"This time, it would have nothing to do with work,"
he said. "And it's a line that probably shouldn't be
crossed."

"You're right about the first part," she said. "The
second thing you said is debatable."

"Are you saying you want me to kiss you as Quint,
not your 'husband'?" he asked.

Rather than answer with words, Ree turned toward
him and pressed her lips to his. The heat in her body
sparked, and a flame burned low in her belly as she
parted her lips for him, and he drove his tongue inside
her mouth.

Her heart raced and her breath quickened as she bit
down on his lower lip. The taste of dark roast coffee
was so much better on Quint.

QUINT REPOSITIONED THE laptop onto the nightstand next
to the bed, breaking apart from kissing Ree for a few
seconds. In those moments, he hoped logic would kick
in and tell them not to ruin what had the potential to be
a great professional partnership. It didn't. In fact, logic
seemed to have walked right out the door and left the
building. Kissing Ree again was an all-consuming need.

Matters weren't helped when she climbed on his lap after he reclaimed his spot on the bed. In the heat of the moment, all he could concentrate on was the feel of her soft lips against his and the sexy little moan of pleasure he swallowed that jacked his pulse up a few more notches. He was consumed by her incredibly silky skin and how it would feel underneath his hands, a ridiculously thin piece of cotton the only thing separating her body from skin-to-skin contact.

"I'd like permission to touch you," he said, his mouth moving against her lips.

She took one of his hands in hers and repositioned it to her full breast. Her nipple beaded with contact, and all blood flew south. Ree brought her hands up to his chest, her fingernails digging into his shoulders as the kisses deepened, and she started rocking back and forth. He dropped his hands to her sweet, round hips as they sped up, and desire flooded him.

In the next moment, she shrugged out of her pajama shirt and tossed it onto the floor. He cupped her incredibly perfect bare breasts in his hands as she released another one of those sexy moans. His T-shirt came off next before he chucked it on top of the pile.

When her gaze met his and locked on, something stirred deep in his chest. There was a second of hesitation on his part because he realized in that moment if this went further there'd be more than a professional partnership on the line. The only question remaining was whether or not his heart could take it. Because making love to Ree would be a game changer. One he wasn't certain he could come back from and just be friends again.

"Are we good?" she asked, her emerald eyes sparkling with need.

Consequences be damned, he said, "Never better."

And then he shifted his weight to remove his jeans and boxers to free his straining erection. In the next couple of seconds, Ree slipped off her pajama bottoms and straddled him. She started to lower her body, but he stopped her.

"What's wrong?" she asked.

"Nothing. I just want to slow down and look at you," he said.

A red blush crawled up her milky skin, concentrating on her cheeks. Blushing made her even more beautiful, if that was possible.

"You are gorgeous," he said, and he could hear the huskiness in his own voice. Being here in this moment with Ree felt like the most natural thing in the world. He had every intention of enjoying each inch of her incredible body.

"I'm not," she said in almost a whisper.

"Then you don't see what I do," he said, smoothing his hands along her hips, moving up and over her stomach until reaching her breasts. Her breaths came in bursts as he touched her, really touched her.

Her back arched as she moaned with pleasure when he dropped his hand to the apex of her thighs. Using the pad of his thumb, he massaged and teased until her eyes were wild with need and he could sense her body ached as much as his.

"Now," she managed to say. "I need you inside me now, Quint."

The sound of his name rolling off her tongue spurred him on. "Hold on a sec."

He retrieved a condom, ripped the package open using his teeth, and then she helped him sheath his stiff length. Once again, she climbed on top of him, straddling him, her sweet heat within inches of absolute ecstasy.

Both hands on her hips, he eased her body down until he was able to dip his tip inside her.

"Quint," she whispered, "more."

He didn't respond. Couldn't respond. All he could do was slow down as much as possible so this whole thing wasn't over before it began. It had been a long time since he'd been with someone who sparked this level of need in him…maybe never. He was both fascinated by it and concerned.

To hell with concern. Right here, right now, he wanted to bury himself inside Ree. She slowly rocked her hips as he kissed her, letting her take the lead. His hands roamed her warm, silky skin.

Game changer all right.

That was the last rational thought he had before giving in to the need scorching his skin and threatening to consume him like a raging wildfire. He surrendered to the feeling, to Ree, and hoped like hell the fire didn't devour them both.

Chapter Nineteen

Ree opened her eyes to a quiet apartment. She felt around for Quint, searching for his warm body. He wasn't there. She heard a noise coming from the living room area, the click-click-clack of fingers on a keyboard. Did this man never sleep?

She lost count of how many rounds of sex they'd had as she stretched out her arms, feeling more relaxed than she had in too long. Waking up after multiple rounds of sex with her work partner should make her feel different…right? Nervous to be around him? Unsure of what this did to their partnership, maybe? Instead, all she could think about was seeing his gorgeous face again. And coffee. Definitely coffee. She'd already let two cups get cold today and, despite not being able to erase the silly smile from her face, needed a caffeine boost.

"Hey," she said after throwing on her robe and walking past him on her way to the kitchen.

"I'd say good morning, but it's a little late for that," he said, shifting the laptop onto the sofa and joining her in the kitchen. He wasted no time kissing her, and a little sense of relief washed over her that he wasn't going to pretend like the last few hours hadn't happened.

"Good afternoon or whatever," she said, looping her arms around his neck as he deepened the kiss and need welled up inside her. How? She'd already had more orgasms today than she could count. How on earth could her body rally, asking for more?

Quint's flat palm splayed against the small of her back caused her stomach to free-fall again. What could she say? The man did things to her body she never knew were possible.

He pulled away first and took a step back, leaning his slender hip against the counter. His shirtless chest was temptation on a stick, but she stopped her fingers from reaching out to him. She had enough time for coffee and an update before she needed to get ready for her shift.

"We got some interesting news," he said as he waited for her to pour her coffee and then take the first sip.

"Oh, yeah?" She gave a little mewl of pleasure that seemed to spark Quint's interest.

"The person Esteban was meeting with has been identified as Constantin's brother Baptiste," he stated.

"It would make sense that Esteban might be running illegal operations, since he's under the government's radar," Ree reasoned.

"Same with Constantin's brother. He isn't listed on any of the company paperwork and flies back and forth to Europe rotating names. He's also been John and Ian," he said.

"Isn't Ian the same thing as John in other countries?" she asked.

Quint rocked his head.

"Let me guess, his nickname is John the Baptist," she said.

"You would be correct. Turns out he likes to dump bodies in rivers," he informed.

Ree shivered. Yes, her job was dangerous, but a lot of times she was busting gunrunners who moved a lot of merchandise at gun shows pretending to be "collectors," which fell under special rules in Texas and didn't require a license, and not this level of evil.

"And he was the one meeting with Esteban?" she asked, already sensing the answer.

"Yes," he confirmed.

"This casts Lola in a whole new light, doesn't it?" she asked.

"If you follow the evidence and take out personal opinion, then yes," he said. "But you know what? Something has been bothering me, and I finally figured out what it is."

She took a sip of coffee, very interested in his revelation. Quint wasn't just a legend at the agency, he was a damn good agent.

"Criminals are usually suspicious of everyone around them," he pointed out. "Right?"

"Seems to come with the territory," she agreed.

"Why wouldn't she have suspected spyware on her laptop?" he asked.

"She was genuinely surprised by the news and looked a little panicked," she admitted.

"Not exactly the actions of an experienced criminal," he stated.

"No, they are not." She took another sip and contemplated the new perspective. "Maybe she'll open up to me a little bit more tonight. I wish I could get her out of the bar for a girls' night out but I'm guessing Constantin keeps a pretty tight grip on her outside of work."

Quint nodded.

"Do you have a picture of Baptiste to show me in case he comes into the bar?" She wanted to know who she was dealing with and be able to monitor who interacted with Lola.

Quint exited the small kitchen, returning a few moments later with the laptop. "The picture is grainy, but here you go."

She memorized his features, which was easy considering he looked like a slightly younger, slightly darker-haired version of his big brother. "I do see the family resemblance."

Quint nodded.

"It's unmistakable," he said.

She took a step closer and pressed a tender kiss to his lips. "Be careful tonight going to Galveston without me." What she really meant to say was "without backup," but figured he probably knew what she was trying to say.

"Always am," he said with a spark in his eyes. "But you can keep kissing me all you want until I fully comprehend the message."

"I keep kissing you and I'll never make it to my shift on time," she stated, and she wasn't kidding. She could stand there and kiss Quint all day long. Since that wasn't an option, she chugged her coffee instead. "In fact, I should probably get ready."

"Killjoy," he said, tugging at her arm as she walked past and he balanced the laptop with his free hand.

"You have no idea how difficult it is for me to go to work today," she said with a smile.

"Same." He dipped his head down and kissed her. It was tender with a hint of so much more. She'd had "so much more" earlier today and had to say that she wouldn't mind a few more rounds.

"We should probably think about getting serious," she said after he pulled back and they both took in a deep breath.

"It may be too late for that," he practically mumbled.

She reminded herself not to ask for clarification as to whether or not he was still talking about work.

Ree dressed in her uniform and returned to the kitchen half an hour later.

"There's a salad in the fridge if you're hungry. I'd volunteer to bring you dinner at work, but I doubt I'll be around," he said. Those words sat a little heavy on her chest. This seemed like a good time to remind herself just how stellar an agent Quint was and how capable he was of taking care of himself in potentially dangerous situations.

"I'm still not thrilled that you'll be going to Galveston without backup," she admitted, pulling a Caesar salad from the fridge.

"It's just me getting the lay of the land. Nothing more. There won't be any engagement," he reassured.

So why was she still stressed about him leaving? Galveston was only a forty-five-minute drive without traffic. He could be there and back before her shift was over. Whatever was bothering her, Ree needed to shake it off.

"ARE YOU READY?" Ree stood in the hallway looking a little too good.

"Let's do this." Quint would be ready to go to Galveston the minute after he returned from walking Ree to the bar. "And don't worry about me. I'll be careful."

"I know you will. You're important to me," she said by way of explanation, giving him a kiss before they headed out the door.

Partners relied on each other in life-and-death situations. Was their personal relationship clouding their objectivity?

Quint didn't want to put a whole lot of stock into the thought as they stepped inside the waiting elevator. Instead, he reached for her hand and entwined their fingers. The move had become habit in a short time, and the link more reassuring than it probably should be.

Neither spoke or seemed to feel the need to fill the air with words. Instead, she squeezed his hand like it was a life raft.

"I could hold off on making the trip if it—"

"No. Go ahead," she reassured him as they hit the lobby floor. "You'll be fine without me."

"You're pretty amazing," he said to her, and meant every word.

"I know." She smirked. The playfulness was back in full force as they walked outside into the Texas heat.

He shook his head and smiled.

Ree nudged him and gave an almost imperceptible nod to the right. He glanced over and, out of the corner of his eye, saw Baptiste holding a little dark-haired girl's hand and walking toward the building. The kid was unmistakable... Lili. She had a small ice-cream cone in her other hand.

He squeezed Ree's hand to acknowledge he saw them. Baptiste the babysitter? This whole scenario didn't sit well.

"Interesting" was all Ree said.

"Isn't it?"

There was no use trying to talk about it here in the open. It did make Quint wonder if he should stick around here rather than head down to Galveston. Then again, this might be exactly the time to make the trip. If Baptiste was here, then Constantin might be as well. Quint could nose around at their home base without too much concern for being caught.

Ree stopped short of the front door of the bar.

"It sure is hot outside today," she said.

"I do feel the temperature heating up," he agreed. There'd been no sign of Matias, so Quint would check to see if Grappell had any intel on his movements.

"Drive safe." She gave him a quick kiss and then a look that stirred something deep in the center of his chest.

"See you at the end of your shift," he promised.

"I'm holding you to that," she said before turning around and walking inside the glass doors.

He saw Lola waving Ree over and figured she was ready to dig into conversation. Again, Lola didn't seem the drug-running, weapons-trading type. Was she that good at fooling people? At tricking him? It had been a long time since anyone had snowed him to that degree. There'd been questionable folks in the past he could put on either side of the equation and not think twice if he'd put them in the wrong bucket.

Maybe Ree could get information from Lola and they could get a break in the case. There were a lot of random dots that needed connecting. The most disturbing piece of information was Baptiste with Lola's daughter.

Quint hoofed it back to the building, truck key in hand. True to Bjorn's word, the vehicle had arrived with new tires this morning. She'd threatened to personally charge him for the expensive set after hearing from the DEA director.

He hopped in the truck and made the drive to Galveston in record time, noting the Fish Shack at the entrance to Constantin's neighborhood. Constantin's home was on the bay side. It was painted a teal blue and looked like something he'd expect to see in Key West, complete with a mounted sailfish hanging on one of the outside walls.

There were no vehicles parked underneath or on the parking pad, which didn't mean no one had eyes on the place. In fact, from where he stood at the house next door, he'd already noted two cameras. Did Constantin live here? This was his address of record. It was possible he had another place in Houston closer to his business that might be rented under someone else's name. His brother's? There could also be a cash-only deal going on without a paper trail. Criminals had plenty of tools at their disposal to help them stay under the radar. A large part of law enforcement was trying to stay one step ahead. Or at the very least not falling too far behind.

There was a light on in the kitchen of Constantin's house and light flickering as though a TV was on. Someone could be there to watch the place. On second thought, the person would most likely have transportation. A housekeeper might make sense. Someone to cook and clean for Constantin and his brother, and basically look after the place while they were gone.

Not much seemed to be going on here, but he pitched a listening device toward the place, nailing a pillar. He moved toward the water, checking for a boat. The main reason to live bayside was to have a place with direct water access. A boat was secured, so nothing to report there. The thought occurred to him to hop into the water and swim over, dropping a listening device and tracker onto the boat. Another set of cameras would make going undetected next to impossible.

Constantin and his brother must stay here at least part of the time. Lola had mentioned going to Galveston on her day off.

Since this trip was turning out to be a dud, he hopped back inside his truck and visited the nearest restaurant. If Constantin wanted to go somewhere for a meeting, the Fish Shack would be the perfect place. It had a dive-bar feel with dim lights and lots of privacy in the booths. The bar took up one side of the place, running along the right wall. A few folks dotted the long counter.

"Table for one?" the twenty-ish hostess asked. "Or will you be sitting at the bar tonight?"

Quint patted down his pockets. "You know what? I just realized that I left my wallet in my truck. I'll be right back."

"Okay." The hostess practically beamed.

Quint walked out, hopped in his truck and got back on the highway running toward the city. There was no use spending much more time in Galveston. This seemed like Constantin's private residence, where he took Lola and Lili, and not where he did business. Good to know. If anything was going on worth knowing here, the listening device should help find it.

The drive home went by fast as Quint turned the radio to a country-and-western station. Randy Travis was on, so Quint rolled down the windows and turned up the sound. As he got closer to his building, he rolled the windows back up, turned off the radio. There was something about a warm late-summer night and the sound of Randy Travis's voice that gave Quint the feeling everything was right in the world.

Or was the feeling coming from the thought that Ree would be off work soon? He parked in their spot and then headed up to the seventh floor. Her shift didn't end for another couple of hours, so he opened the laptop and grabbed a power bar to tide him over while he fiddled around.

Esteban's connection to Constantin and Baptiste wasn't a stretch. After all, Lola and Constantin were in a serious relationship. Matias's being in Houston shouldn't surprise anyone considering he was Lili's father. Quint made a note in the case file asking if Matias had been involved with Lili her entire life or if he'd recently found out about his daughter. He wished he could just ask Lola outright, but getting too personal would look suspicious. He'd won some trust by telling her about the spyware. There was no need to blow it now.

Quint requested as much DEA information about Matias as they were willing to give. Somehow, he doubted Driver would pony up information, but Shelly might see the question. She'd made it clear she wanted to cooperate and didn't share her partner's views. In fact, she was the one person who seemed more put off by having to work with Driver than they were. Rightfully so. As much as Driver annoyed Quint, at least they weren't partners. He couldn't imagine working side by side with Wonder Boy.

That being said, Quint figured he could ask Ree to reach out to Shelly now that her number was on Ree's cell phone. The numbers were phantom if anyone tried to trace them from the outside. They would link to a made-up identity.

Quint took a power nap before freshening up and heading out to the bar. Once there, he stood, arms crossed, leaning against a barricade blocking vehicles from driving in front of the pedestrian area and glanced around. Constantin sat in his Lamborghini, the engine idling. Either the transport business was incredibly lucrative, or crime paid. His money was on the latter.

Lola stepped out with Ree, who smiled at him the second she spotted him. There was something extra special about her smile tonight. A piece of him wanted it to be about what had happened earlier between them. Instinct said she got information from Lola. Then again, maybe it was both. He could only hope that was true. Either way, he was about to find out.

Chapter Twenty

The minute Ree made eye contact with Quint, her chest squeezed, and she was filled with warmth.

"Bye," she said to Lola, who waved before getting into the bright yellow sports car. Seriously? If Ree had the kind of money to spend on a vehicle like that she most certainly wouldn't buy one that was highlighter yellow. Constantin might have good taste in girlfriends, but that was where it ended.

Quint hauled her against his chest and kissed her. Properly. Thoroughly.

"The first kiss was for me," he whispered, his lips so close to her ear she could feel his warm breath. A sensitized skitter ran the length of her neck.

He linked their fingers and held tight as they made the trek back to the apartment. Once inside, he went straight to the fridge while she changed into something more comfortable.

"How did it go in Galveston?" she asked.

He gave a quick rundown.

"Did you find out anything new at work?"

"It was far too busy to talk," Ree said with disappointment in her voice.

Quint muttered a curse.

"I need to do laundry tomorrow before work," she said as a knock sounded at the door. Her heart galloped as she walked over to the door and then checked the peephole. She opened the door to Angie. "Hey. Everything okay?"

"It's late, I know," Angie started, balancing two glasses of wine in her hands. "Can I come in? I brought alcohol."

"Um, yeah, sure. Why not," Ree said, stumbling a little bit. She took a step back. "Come on in."

"I can run down and throw in a load of laundry while the two of you talk," Quint said.

"You'd do my laundry?" Ree asked, not bothering to mask her shock. And then she realized that might sound funny coming from a married woman.

Angie must have been in her own world, because she walked on in and plopped down on the sofa, setting the wineglasses down on the coffee table. Ree shot a look toward Quint, and he smiled.

He mouthed the words *no worries*. "I'll heat up your plate of leftovers and bring it into the living room. Looks like Angie needs to talk."

"Thank you, honey," she said before walking over and planting a sweet kiss on his lips.

"Save more of that for later," he said with a wink that brought on a serious smile. The man was gorgeous and funny. He was smart and could handle himself in pretty much any situation. Her heart needed Bubble

Wrap for the damage a person like that could do given direct access. Was it too late?

"What happened?" Ree asked as she turned to face Angie and headed into the living room.

"I heard your door open, so I knew you'd be up. I hope this is okay," Angie said. Her face twisted in distress.

"Totally fine," Ree said, taking a seat. "It would have been totally unacceptable without the wine, though."

Angie laughed. Quint brought over a warm plate of food and set it on the coffee table before excusing himself. All hope there would be a sexual repeat of this afternoon died as Angie settled in.

"What's wrong?" Ree asked.

"This test is going to be the death of me," Angie whined. "It's so stressful and my parents will kill me if I don't get a decent score. Do you know how proud of me they sounded when I told them I was going to apply to law school?"

"I'm sure they'll understand," Ree pointed out. "You've been studying your behind off."

Angie kicked into her version of life with her parents and their expectations as Quint slipped out the door with a bag of laundry in his hands.

QUINT HAD ONE of those eyes-on-him feelings as he exited the elevator and then opened the door to the laundry room. He'd turned around twice only to find an empty hallway. He was either becoming paranoid or starting to second-guess himself. Neither was good for his line of work. His backup weapon was tucked neatly inside his ankle holster and within easy reach, he thought as the hairs on the back of his neck pricked.

He loaded up the washer, bought soap from the vending machine and turned around to find Baptiste standing in the doorway. There was no chance this was a coincidence. And Quint realized it because Baptiste wasn't carrying any laundry. The fact that the man leered at Quint was another clue. There were no weapons in Baptiste's hands, so that was probably a good sign he didn't intend to take Quint out of this room in a body bag.

"Need to borrow any soap?" Quint asked, sizing his opponent up. Baptiste was considerably smaller in stature, but Quint would put money on the younger man being surprisingly strong. There was something about his wiry build that said he was scrappy. His nose had been broken at least twice. There was a sizable scar above his left cheek.

"No." The one-word answer revealed a thick accent.

"Mind if I continue, then?" Quint asked, using the stall tactic to size up his opponent. As it was, he was going to have to walk in front of Baptiste to get to the washer on the other side of the room.

Baptiste shrugged. "Don't mind me."

Quint took in a breath and crossed the room. He dug his thumbnail into the packet of laundry soap, creating a sizable hole that he kept plugged with said thumb.

As predicted, Baptiste threw a punch and bumrushed Quint all at once. Quint unplugged the soap and flung it into Baptiste's eyes. He yelled a few choice words as he threw a shoulder into Quint, driving him into a stacked dryer unit. He came up with an elbow to the face and heard a snap when he made contact. Another broken nose? This guy was about to get even uglier. Up close, he already had the marks of a professional boxer.

Baptiste drew up his knee but Quint hopped out of the way just in time, having anticipated the move. As Baptiste blinked what must be blurry, burning eyes, Quint emptied the rest of the soap there.

The move caused Baptiste to scream out in pain and throw a flurry of punches. One of them connected to Quint's jaw, another to his nose.

"What's your problem exactly?" Quint asked, countering with a punch to Baptiste's rib cage.

The man doubled over and dropped down to his knees. Quint kicked him with the toe of his boot before walking away and buying another packet of laundry detergent as Baptiste regrouped.

"Don't you ever look at the little girl I was with earlier again," he finally spit out.

"Or what?" Quint asked as he walked past the man and then loaded his soap into the machine. "You'll do what to me?"

"Not just me… My brother will make certain you never walk again." Baptiste rubbed red eyes as he nodded toward Quint's ankles.

"Yeah? Tell your brother that his threats don't scare me and I'll look at anyone I damn well please," Quint said through clenched teeth. He'd taken a punch that was going to hurt later once the adrenaline wore off. Frustration burned through him. "But for the record,

I don't give a rat's... Let's just say little girls don't do anything for me."

"Tell that bitch of a wife of yours to watch it," Baptiste said as he backpedaled toward the door. "She's poking around where she doesn't belong."

"How about this instead? Mind your own damn business. My wife can speak to whomever she wants, whenever she wants. She's a grown woman who can think for herself." Quint felt the trickle of blood from his own nose and figured there'd be some explaining to do when he got home. "And if anything happens to this laundry, I'll know exactly where to look."

Baptiste hesitated at the door. He'd underestimated Quint. It wouldn't happen again. Next time, if there was one, Baptiste would be more prepared.

"Hear what I said" was all Baptiste said before turning to walk away.

Quint made his way back to the apartment, needing to stem the nosebleed. He walked into the apartment after unlocking the door and went straight into the kitchen, hoping the distraction in the next room would stop Ree from figuring out what had just happened. She'd had a bad feeling earlier today, and he didn't want to worry her. But make no mistake about it, Quint considered himself warned by Constantin.

His first thought was that Constantin knew about the trip to Galveston, but Baptiste hadn't mentioned anything about it. He'd been concerned about the little girl. As much as Quint wanted to give the guy a medal for his "genuine" concern, he recognized a threat when he received one.

"Hey, honey," Ree said in a subtle tone that said she needed to be rescued.

"I'll be right there," he said, wadding up a few paper towels before pressing them to his nose. He blotted the towel and realized there was a small cut on the side of his nose. He made a move to go to the bathroom but got caught halfway there.

"Honey?" Ree said.

"Bathroom" was all he said. "It's a nosebleed. The weather must be changing."

"I get those, too," Angie said, clearly having had some wine. "It's how I know the seasons are about to turn."

Quint didn't look over, and to Ree that would be suspicious as hell. Angie kept prattling on about living a lie and how hard it was not being honest with her parents, how she was about to fail the LSAT, and how they'd blame her boyfriend if they ever found out about the living arrangement, which clearly they would at some point. She seemed certain of it.

"If they love you, they'll understand if you get a bad score," Ree reassured her, but she was drowning.

"I don't know," Angie said. "They're so judgmental and have such high expectations of me. I feel like I disappoint them all the time."

"I bet they're proud of you," Ree said, but there was no conviction in her voice. Was she reminded of her own family's disapproval of her job? Of her mother's disappointment in having a daughter who didn't turn out to be the person she'd hoped?

"Maybe," Angie said.

"And you know what? Who cares if they aren't?" Ree finally said, and he had to fight the urge to go into the next room and cheer. Ree was an intelligent, kind, funny and beautiful woman inside and out. How any mother wouldn't burst with pride at having Ree as her daughter was beyond him.

He grabbed his first aid kit out of the cabinet and checked the mirror. The cut wasn't bad. Thankfully, the cut wasn't on top of his head. Those could make a person think they needed a trip to the ER for how much blood came out of the tiniest nick.

After cleaning himself up, he figured hopping in the shower might give Angie the hint to leave. Fifteen minutes later, he joined Ree and their company in the living room.

"I'll grab the laundry," he said as Angie stood up. Her wineglass was empty, as was Ree's, and the tension in Angie's face was gone.

"I should go," Angie said, picking up both glasses.

"I'll walk you out," Quint offered.

At the door, Ree touched his forearm. Her gaze lingered on the cut on his nose. He gave a slight nod.

"I'll come to the laundry with you," Ree offered. "Meet you at the elevator?"

"Sounds like a plan." He realized instantly that she'd caught on and was going for her weapon.

Angie split, heading into her apartment. Quint held off on pushing the elevator button. At this time of night, it wouldn't be difficult to get one. Ree joined him a minute later. She hid her waist holster well, but he knew what to look for.

After linking their fingers, he retrieved the elevator. A car waited on their floor, so the bell dinged immediately. It was the same car he'd used a short while ago, and probably a good sign there hadn't been any activity since. He'd feel even better if this was the only elevator.

The walk down the hallway had him tightening his grip on Ree's hand. A few steps before the laundry room door, he filled her in on what had happened before he let go of her fingers so they'd be ready to pull a weapon in a heartbeat should the need arise. Quint figured being ready for Baptiste had given him all the advantage he'd needed to dispatch the threat. Being caught off guard always put someone at a disadvantage. His ribs were feeling the pain from a few of those jabs. His face hurt. But he was alive and kicking, and nothing had happened that a good night of sleep and an ibuprofen couldn't cure.

"Washer's done," he said as they entered the quiet room. Ree went right and he went left as though they'd practiced this routine a hundred times. When her side of the room was cleared, she gave the hand signal. He did the same before they reunited at the washer with her clothes inside. She was quiet as she worked and he could tell she was processing the information about him being attacked.

Together, they moved the load into the dryer, checking each piece for signs a listening device had been planted. He doubted it and, based on her expression, so did she. It was important to consider every possibility.

They sat in silence while the dryer spun the clothes around, keeping an eye toward the door just in case.

He used a washer as a backrest as she leaned against him. He looped his arms around her, clasping his hands. She stood, back to his chest. Quint could stand like this forever.

The dryer stopped, so they emptied it, draping clothes over their arms so they wouldn't wrinkle.

Once back inside the apartment, Ree immediately said, "I'll take care of these." She shooed him away. "Now, tell me everything that happened with Baptiste in the laundry room."

He sat on the edge of the bed.

"Nothing too terrible happened. He didn't like the fact that I saw him with Lili earlier in the day," he said. "Then he warned me about you getting too close to Lola."

"I've been wanting to tell you something all night but Angie was here," Ree stated. "Constantin takes Lola to Galveston on her days off like we assumed. Constantin has his own place near here, though. It's a house, and he's been pressuring Lola to move in with him. She's been holding off, says she isn't certain he's 'the one,' but I can tell it's something else. There's something about her disposition that changes when she talks about him."

"She did just find out he was most likely spying on her via her laptop," he pointed out.

"That's true," she said. "And a very good observation. It might be the stress of realizing her boyfriend doesn't trust her that causes tension in her face muscles now when she talks about him. I have nothing to compare her reactions to since the subject didn't come up before she learned the news."

Quint nodded.

"Learning your boyfriend is spying doesn't exactly help if there are any trust issues in the first place," he added.

"True again," she agreed.

"What about Esteban?" he asked. "Were you able to get information about him?"

"Only that he does work for Constantin sometimes, and that information didn't come directly from Lola, by the way. He stopped by the bar and seemed to be frustrated about something. I overheard that Esteban is basically being blackmailed into running these 'special errands' as he called them," she informed him.

"He wants nothing to do with Constantin's business?" he asked.

"Absolutely not," she confirmed. "He said he wasn't sure how long he could keep doing it.

"Her response came immediately," she said. "She told him there was no choice."

"Sounds like Constantin is holding Esteban's illegal status over his head," Quint reasoned. He'd seen it before in past cases. Some folks were just born bad, ready to embrace the wrong side of the law. Others were brought to it by environment, growing up in a rough family situation, neighborhood or both. Then there were those who came to it by circumstance, a quick need for money and the feeling there was no other alternative, or, like in Esteban's case, blackmail.

"My mind went there, too," she admitted as she hung

up her work blouse. "And that could be another reason why there's tension in her relationship with Constantin. She might not have known what she was getting into with him when they first started dating. Now, though, she's figuring out the real him, and it's not looking good."

"Knowing Constantin's business also makes it more difficult to leave him, and she would realize that he wouldn't want any loose ends running around. Also, the fact that Matias is in town complicates life for Lola and possibly Esteban," Quint noted. "I'd like to find out from the other team when he arrived in Houston, how frequently he shows up here and if they have a sense of when he might leave.

"Can you reach out to Shelly and find out everything she knows about Matias? There's not enough in the file to go on or give us any real insight into the man," Quint said.

"Lola doesn't like talking about him," Ree said.

"I've never met a person who enjoyed bringing up their past mistakes," he stated.

Ree nodded. "I'll shoot a text to Shelly while we're thinking about it." She hung up the last of the clothes and retrieved her phone. She sent the text and then set her phone on the nightstand, giving him a look that said things were about to get interesting between them. "Maybe we'll hear back by morning."

Quint shrugged out of his T-shirt as Ree climbed onto the bed, toward him.

Her cell phone picked that moment to interrupt them.

Chapter Twenty-One

On a sharp sigh, Ree backpedaled and grabbed her cell from the nightstand. Shelly. "That was fast."

"What did she say?" Quint asked.

"Word is that Matias is planning to duck out of the country. He's acting nervous and jumpy, and they want to move on him soon," she said.

"Wait. Hold on a minute. If they move on Matias, our investigation is done." Quint grabbed his shirt and his phone. "We can't allow that to happen."

"The department heads will work together—"

"No, the DEA will walk all over Bjorn, and I can't risk losing this trail toward Dumitru," Quint countered.

"No one is losing anything yet." Ree tried to inject some calm into a situation that had gone from DEF-CON level five to one in two seconds. She read the rest of the text. "Arresting him once he leaves the country is that much more difficult, so Nick is pushing to act as soon as possible. Word of warning, he will move in the second he gets clearance."

Ree texted back asking how soon that might be. The response came almost immediately.

"Okay, so, it's looking like it could literally be any moment. We should probably be hearing from Bjorn soon and the DEA is 'promising' to give us as much warning as they can." Ree formed actual air quotes with her fingers when she said the word *promising*.

"We all know how this goes down. They won't give us a heads-up until they're on their way to the bust, seconds before making it, or done. All our work up to this point goes up in smoke." Quint fisted his left hand, and she figured he didn't even realize he was doing it. He white-knuckled his cell phone.

"Hold on. Shelly is typing again," Ree said. The message came through. "She doesn't think it'll go down before tomorrow night, if that helps at all."

"It does," Quint stated through clenched teeth. "We have less than twenty-four hours to figure out our case or get preempted by Wonder Boy over there."

Ree thanked Shelly for the information and the heads-up.

Ree said to Quint, "At least we know.

"What are the chances we can stay in place after the drug bust?" she asked, knowing it was too risky because everyone around Lola would be scrutinized. Since Ree's employment at the bar coincided with the bust, there was no way she wouldn't be suspect. At the very least, she would be scrutinized. It wouldn't be good for her or the case they were building against Constantin. Something dawned on her. "We must be getting close ourselves."

"How so?" Quint's eyebrow arched.

"What happened in the laundry room earlier. There's

no way we would be sent a warning if Constantin and his brother were comfortable. Right?" she asked, snapping her fingers together. "We struck a nerve by me getting close to Lola."

"There's no way Baptiste saw me gawking at Lili, since I wasn't," he said. "I barely looked in their direction."

"Constantin is getting overly protective because…"

"I doubt they picked me up on their cameras in Galveston, because that was one of my first thoughts," he said, brainstorming out loud.

"If they did, it sure was fast," she said.

"There were a whole lot of cameras around the actual residence in Galveston. It didn't occur to me they could be on the neighborhood entrance as well," he reasoned.

"Baptiste didn't bring it up, though. He focused on Lili and Lola," she said.

"He might not have wanted to show his hand on the Galveston residence," he admitted. "There's a chance he might not have wanted me to know they saw the truck."

"I'm sure Constantin is keeping tabs on the building," she said. "We're new tenants. I work with Lola."

"All true," he said. "You have a few things going for you in that you let Angie take the lead of creating a friendship."

"That's probably why Lola doesn't suspect me of anything," she admitted. "But Constantin and his brother would pick up on those other things.

"Lola jumped at the chance to bring her laptop to

you," Ree said. "Did that mean she was looking for a friend or a way out?"

"Too bad we can't march up to the ninth floor and ask," Quint stated.

"Wait a minute. That's a really good idea actually," Ree said.

"It's too risky. I've already been told to keep you away from Lola," Quint warned.

"Not me." Ree pointed next door. "Angie has a habit of showing up at people's doors, sometimes with wineglasses in hand."

"Or possibly coffee," he said. "Then again, Angie was headed to a coffee shop yesterday morning to study. Maybe she could get Lola out of the building. We could talk to her outside of here if Angie can get Lola out of the building without a tail. Maybe get a better feel for where Lola's head is in all this. Her brother wants a way out. The two seem close."

"Think we can get a message to Esteban?" she asked.

"I doubt it, and it would be too risky. We don't exactly know what his involvement is in all this," he said. "He might not want to work for Constantin, but that doesn't mean the guy is in the clear in my book."

"Right." Ree's cell buzzed again, indicating another text had come through. She grabbed her phone and checked the screen. "You've got to be kidding me."

"What?" Quint patted the bed in the spot next to him.

Ree moved beside him. "Shelly just warned us to keep an eye on our tires if we want to go anywhere tomorrow."

Quint was up and off that bed in the space of a heartbeat. Ree quickly followed, jumping in between him and the path to the door just in case he got any ideas. Instead, he started pacing. "That son of a bi—"

Ree put both hands up in the surrender position. "I know, but we need to be smart about how we handle this information."

"It was a so-called drug deal at the warehouse," Quint continued. "The 'dealer' had to be connected somehow to Wonder Boy as maybe an informant."

"That makes the most sense," she reasoned as anger heated the blood in her veins to the boiling point. Still, she managed to keep it together long enough to thank Shelly. "She is taking a big risk in telling us this."

"I know" was all Quint said.

"Lola gave me her phone number at the bar tonight," Ree said. "I forgot to mention that earlier."

"That could be what prompted the laundry room visit," he reasoned.

"True," she agreed. "Shelly could get into a whole lot of trouble sharing this with us, so please don't go storming up to Nick and give him a black eye even though he deserves it."

"I'm angry, not stupid. There's no way I'm giving him the satisfaction of taking my badge, even if it's just for a suspension, because of his actions," Quint said.

"Agreed." Ree circled the opposite way as she paced. Twice they almost collided, stopping for a second before sidestepping and moving on.

"The only question in my mind is, what are we going to do about it?" Quint said.

ALL QUINT COULD see was red. It was a hue that colored everything in the room, including Ree as she passed by. On her, however, it looked good. Hell, everything looked good on Ree.

"You're right about one thing, though," he said.

"Which is?" she asked as they looped past, making another round.

"I really want to punch the smug bastard," he said.

"He got us over a barrel with Bjorn," Ree stated.

"Damn right he did." More of that anger threatened to break through. He'd been managing it so far, but that didn't mean the teakettle wasn't about to boil over. "He put us exactly in the position he wanted, and now our hands are tied as to standing down while he takes over his side of the bust."

Ree stopped him midpace. She checked the time, which confused him.

"Is there anything that can be done about this in the next fifteen to twenty minutes?" she asked.

"Other than come up with a plan as to how we're going to take that bastard down and still protect our case?" he asked.

"All I see is red and I can't think clearly." She smoothed her flat palm over his chest. "But I can think of a great way to burn off some of this energy so we can."

That was pretty much all the encouragement Quint needed. In the next few seconds, hands roamed and at some point clothes ended up in a pile on the floor. Their bodies ended up a tangle in the sheets. And his heart ended up taking a huge hit.

After an incredible round of making love, she fell asleep in his arms. Quint followed soon after.

He had no idea how many hours had passed by the time he opened his eyes again.

"I'll make coffee this time," Ree said, peeling off the covers.

He wrapped his arm tighter around her. "Or we could just stay here. It'll only take a few seconds for me to be ready for another round."

Ree laughed. "At this rate, we'll never get out of bed."

"Sounds like a good plan to me," he said.

"But coffee first," she said, pushing against her restraints—his arms. "And then I promise you can have your way with me as much as you like."

"I'll make sure you keep your promise," he said.

"Oh, did I just hear Quint Casey make something that sounded like a commitment?" she said, clearly teasing, and yet the words struck like a physical blow. Was that what was happening here? And why did those words make him want to run in the opposite direction? Being with her in bed felt like the most natural thing in the world. Why did a few words hit him like a pole to the chest at a hundred miles an hour?

He mumbled something as he let go of her and then grabbed his clothes out of the pile. She sat on the edge of the bed for a long moment, silent. This was probably where he should say something to her that would explain the situation or how he truly felt about her. Except no words came. The only thing he knew for certain was that he cared about her more than he had anyone in a very long time. Maybe ever. But what did that mean for their partnership?

Relationships could come and go. Finding the perfect partner was a whole lot rarer. Quint sighed as he slipped on his T-shirt, boxers and then jeans, one leg at a time.

"We have to get Lola alone" was all he said as he crossed the room with his laptop. "Let's see. I haven't checked this in a while, so…"

He booted up the system after setting the device on the counter.

"Send her an email," Ree suggested, her tone clipped. Her back was to him as she made coffee.

Could he explain himself? Smooth things over with her? The last thing he wanted to do was make the situation worse.

"Think we could get to Lili?" he asked.

"It's possible," she said.

And then it dawned on him. "Why didn't I think about this earlier? Matias is about to leave, and suddenly Lili is at Baptiste's side. I'd bet money he and Constantin are protecting her because they realize Matias is about to bolt."

"That would explain Lola's nerves at the bar all night and possibly her discussion with her brother," she said. "Now that I really think about it, I think she told him to hang on a little while longer."

"She could be the key to all this," he stated. "She would do anything to keep her daughter safe."

"Are you suggesting we blackmail her into testifying?" Ree asked.

"It wouldn't be the first time a government agency

used a kid to get someone to testify, but no," he said. "I'm proposing we get her alone and offer her protection if she's willing to go to court for us as a witness."

"Esteban has seen the inner workings of Constantin's business," she said with a nod. The coffee maker finished doing its job, so she turned her back to him and poured two cups of black coffee. When she turned around, her face was unreadable. "Here you go."

"Thank you," he said, taking the offering.

"Based on the conversation with Lola, Esteban wants to be free of running errands for Constantin," Ree said.

"Which doesn't necessarily mean he's not a criminal," Quint said. "But his sister and niece could be incentive to take the offering of a fresh start."

"You said Lola exchanges emails with her mother," Ree said. "How would that work exactly? Lola is all about her family, based on what I've seen so far."

"There's no father in the picture," he said. "I could take a request to Bjorn for the mother to be relocated along with Lola, her daughter and brother."

"You think our boss would go for it?" she asked.

"We won't know if we don't try." He opened the case file, and there it was. The report that said the DEA was about to close their case. Quint bit back a curse.

"What is it?" Ree asked.

"It's official." He turned the screen around to her so she could read it for herself. "The file was uploaded half an hour ago."

"At least Shelly gave us a heads-up it was coming," she said.

"And the knowledge that her partner was not to be trusted on any level," he stated.

"Do you think Bjorn would go to bat for us? Ask for a little more time?" Ree asked.

"Not after the truck incident. She's already angry with me," he said. Quint exhaled slowly. "Not unless we can give her a damn good reason without throwing Shelly under the bus."

Ree took a sip of coffee.

"I might have an angle," she said.

"I'm all ears." Quint hoped the idea had teeth to it. He wanted to bring down Constantin and his brother more than ever, and before the DEA could make their move.

Chapter Twenty-Two

"Do you think we could get Agent Grappell to rush a warrant?" Ree asked, stuffing down the hurt from their earlier conversation in order to focus on the case again. "All we need is access to the warehouse. You could go in as a distraction."

"Constantin could lie. Say he had no knowledge of what was going in and out of that warehouse. It doesn't directly tie him to any crime," Quint pointed out.

"It would be enough to arrest him. While he's detained, I'd have time to work on Lola to see if I can convince her to testify," Ree stated.

"Are you suggesting we go behind Bjorn's back?" he asked.

"Not so much behind her back as doing our jobs without telling her first. We do that all the time," Ree said. "You know how these investigations go. Sometimes things have to move quickly."

"What about the DEA? Matias will get spooked if we go for an arrest with Constantin and Baptiste," Quint said.

"All I can do is ask Shelly to give us a heads-up

moments before the arrest goes down," she said. "I trust her."

"We'd have to in order to pull this off. A simultaneous arrest?" he asked. "There could be a lot of moving parts."

"However, what are the chances Matias is going to be in the same location as Constantin?" she asked.

"Good point there," he said. "Okay, I'll see what Grappell thinks."

Quint grabbed his cell phone and made the call. Phone calls like this happened on cases from time to time when judges had to be awakened for warrants. Time was of the essence in this case. The thought of wrapping it up and moving on from Quint to let him chase Dumitru crossed Ree's mind. Was she getting in too deep on a personal level with Quint? These things happened, too. The intensity of an investigation coupled with the fact that two people were relying on each other in life-and-death situations caused people to sometimes confuse that with true intimacy. Those in-the-heat-of-the-moment relationships always fizzled out, leaving the partnership all kinds of awkward. Agents sometimes asked to be reassigned to work with different partners, and the gossip mill usually figured out the reason. It always came back to a romantic relationship.

How could Ree have been so naive?

She wasn't, a little voice in the back of her mind pointed out. She was falling in love. Two totally different things. Once the partnership was over, the couple would be, too.

Quint ended the call and gave a thumbs-up signal. "Grappell will text when he has the warrant secured."

"Good." It was the only word that came to mind despite feeling the exact opposite. "Do you think this can all go down while I'm at work tonight? It's Thursday, so the shift will be busy, but I should still be able to pull Lola aside, especially if I get there early."

"You've made good progress with her in a short timeframe," he said.

"I think she sees me as a friend," Ree said. "I just hope we're turning her world upside down for good reason."

"Putting a dangerous criminal behind bars is always a good reason," Quint pointed out.

Ree nodded. In theory, she knew it was true. But Lola had come to this country presumably to build a better life for her daughter. Her brother came along, too. Again, her mind snapped to him wanting a better life.

Quint was busy typing up the request to have someone at the ready in Argentina at Lola's mother's house to grab her for witness protection. Knowing her mother was secure and coming to America might sweeten the pot for Lola. Why a woman like her would have gotten mixed up with a jerk like Constantin was beyond Ree. And then the reason dawned on her.

"This is just a guess, but hear me out," Ree started.

He stopped typing and glanced up. The second he saw the seriousness in her eyes, his expression morphed and he sat a little straighter.

"Something we said earlier resonates with me," she began. "Lola would do anything for Lili, right?"

"I believe so," he stated. "From everything we've seen and heard she's a caring mother who is doing her best to protect the little girl from her father..."

Quint's eyes sparked as Ree held up her index finger.

"What you're saying is Lola's relationship with Constantin was always a business transaction for her," he said.

"A way to keep her daughter safe from a guy like Matias, who could potentially grab Lili and take her back to Argentina," Ree reasoned.

"So, Lola meets a bigger criminal and, being beautiful, easily brings him into her life as her boyfriend. He's serious about her, but she's the one holding out because she doesn't love him," Quint stated.

"And never did," Ree added.

"But she's stuck now because Matias is always looming," he continued. "And always a threat."

"Constantin even brings her brother into the 'family' business as a show of trust," Ree said.

"It makes perfect sense to me," Quint stated.

"This is truly my first hope she'll listen to me and go into WITSEC. We can give her and Esteban a new identity," Ree said.

"In my experience, people from other countries living here illegally don't exactly trust American law enforcement," Quint said.

"That's a barrier we'll have to overcome with her," she said. "I strongly believe that if we convince Lola to take the deal in exchange for her and Esteban's testimony, she can convince her brother to go along with the plan. He wants out anyway. Even if he lies low for a couple of years, he'll be able to go anywhere he wants and do anything once he has permanent citizenship."

"She might have a difficult time turning on Constantin. We have no idea how loyal she is. He's been protecting her and Lili for at least a couple of years now," Quint pointed out. "She might not be able to bring herself to turn against him."

"That's the risk we take," Ree said. "But I don't see a whole lot of options if you want to bring this bastard down."

"This is the equivalent of a Hail Mary touchdown," he mumbled.

"Bigger miracles have happened," she responded.

He looked like he was about to open his mouth to speak as the air in the room changed. Since she wasn't ready to talk about "them" and she feared he'd spring the whole "it's not you, it's me" bit on her, she figured she'd save him the time.

"I think we've talked enough for one night, don't you?" she asked as his mouth clamped shut.

"Okay," he said.

"So let's just go to our respective corners and take a little time to figure out what we need to do to wrap this case in a big bow," she continued.

"Okay," he said.

"Fine," she commented. "And don't say *okay* again."

His lips compressed into a thin line. His expression said he was holding back what he really wanted to say. His face told her the news wouldn't be good for her. There was no reason to take that bullet while they needed to plan the next few hours.

QUINT SAT AT the counter while Ree took the sofa. There was so much he needed to say to her, but she was right about one thing. Now wasn't the time.

He spent the rest of the night mapping out a plan and lining up resources with Grappell. A couple of agents mobilized, planning to meet up at the warehouse ten minutes after Ree's shift started at four o'clock. As for Matias, Quint couldn't care less what happened on that side of the bust. Ree was right. The two wouldn't cross over because the likelihood Matias and Constantin would be in the same room was almost zero. Unless, of course, Quint factored in the bar.

Speaking of which, he intended to follow Constantin after he dropped off Lola, because he wanted to personally make that arrest. Baptiste would be under surveillance as well. He would most likely be at the Galveston house or Houston home. Quint's money was on the place closest to here while Matias was in town. In fact, it wouldn't surprise Quint if Matias stayed in Lola's apartment while she worked. It made the most sense when he really thought about it. Baptiste seemed to have an eye for movement in the building and was in charge of keeping watch over Lili at least part of the time.

His cell started dinging over the next few hours as assets moved into place. There would be four agents at the warehouse to make arrests and confiscate equipment. Quint had every intention of being the one to put cuffs on Constantin. Bonus if he got to arrest Baptiste as well. An agent was assigned to work with Quint.

It wasn't lost on him that Ree would be tucked safely

away at the bar while the arrests went down. In order
to be able to hold on to Constantin, they needed Lola's
agreement to testify. In many respects, Ree's job was
going to be the linchpin in their whole operation.

Out of courtesy, he intended to send Shelly a text
before everything went down. Bjorn might be involved
on the back end, so the notice might be too little, too
late on his part. But he planned to do it anyway out of
courtesy for Shelly giving them a heads-up. Arrests
would be timed in the order of Constantin and Baptiste,
then the warehouse. Any other order and Constantin
and Baptiste would likely disappear. The warehouse
had to be timed last.

The day was long and the apartment was quiet save
for the click-click-clack of the keyboard or the occasional cell phone buzz, indicating a message had come
through. Meals came and went. Information was ex-
changed. And then it was time to walk Ree to work.

"When this is over, I'd like a few minutes of your
time," he said to Ree before they walked out the door.

"I think we've said enough to each other, don't
you?" she asked. "And don't worry, I know this case
is a stepping-stone to what you really want, which is
Dumitru. You don't have to show up to my mother's
ranch to convince me to sign on. Just give me a couple
of days to get my head on straight so I can get some
distance and think clearly again."

"Are you sure that's what you want?" he asked, wishing for a different answer but resigned.

"Never been more certain of anything in my life,"
she said. "I've been thinking a lot about what you said

before. People in this job can end up jaded and lonely if they don't make time for a personal life. When this is all over, I plan to prioritize finding that."

Before he could say a word, she grabbed the door handle and walked into the hallway. Angie popped her head out.

"Hey. How are my favorite neighbors today?" She practically beamed.

"That's one big smile you have on your face," Ree said, artfully dodging the subject of the two of them.

"I took your advice and told my parents about my fireman," Angie said.

"Yeah? I'm guessing by the smile on your face they took it well," Ree stated.

"Oh, not at first. But then they came to the realization that I'm a grown adult and in love." She flashed her left hand, and there was a sparkling rock on a certain finger.

"You got engaged?" Ree asked. When she turned, a tear ran down her cheek. It seemed to catch her off guard. She quickly thumbed it away and brought Angie into an embrace. "I'm so happy for you."

"LSAT be damned. My fireman said a score on a test wouldn't make him love me any more or less. I knew right then he was the one." Angie's smile could light the building in a blackout.

Quint offered his congratulations along with a brief hug. "The fireman is one lucky guy."

"You two have to come to my wedding," Angie said with more energy than a Chihuahua after licking a bowl of espresso.

"We'd love to," Ree said, thumbing away another tear.

He'd seen it before. This job, the isolation, the lack of a "normal" life. It could get to a person after a while. Had it gotten to Ree?

"I better get to work," Ree said, "but I'm expecting an invite later."

"How about a glass of wine tonight to celebrate?" Angie asked.

"Rain check?" Ree asked.

"You bet." A little bit of Angie's bubble burst. She really was a good kid who deserved everything in life. Quint reminded himself that people like her were the reason he did this job in the first place. It had sounded corny when he spoke the words out loud in the past, but that didn't make them any less true.

"I'll see you later," Ree promised. She paused after taking a couple of steps toward the elevator. "Do me a favor tonight?"

"Sure. Anything," Angie responded.

"Stay inside your apartment. Binge-watch Netflix. Just tonight," Ree said.

"Okayyy." Angie had no idea why she was agreeing based on the look on her face, but she was a person of her word.

"I want to hear all about what you watched tomorrow at breakfast," Ree said, knowing full well she and Quint would be long gone by then. He doubted they would even come back to this apartment after the bust. One of the other agents would come in and clean up for them, sweeping the place and packing up their stuff, which would "magically" show up at the office tomorrow morning.

After this, Quint intended to take a few days off to regroup and catch his breath before the next case. And there would be a next case. He didn't know how long it would take to get an in with the next rung on the ladder, but it would happen. It was a shame his certainty about life ended there and not with Ree.

Chapter Twenty-Three

Lola was already at work by the time Quint dropped Ree off at the bar. Agent Miguel Brown had been assigned to work the arrest with Quint. Brown was a solid agent and a lucky draw. The two had worked together a few times and had a good rapport.

Brown followed Constantin back to his Houston house. There was one hiccup. He had both his brother and Lili with him, which meant the two of them must know Matias was about to flee the country again. It also stood to reason that Matias wanted to take his daughter with him. Thus, the double protection.

The other complication was the fact that Wonder Boy might be staking out Constantin's house, since it seemed likely Matias would show there. None of this fell into the category of *warm and fuzzy* for Quint except for the fact that Ree would be twenty minutes away at the bar working on Lola.

Quint jogged back to his truck and then hopped into the driver's seat after checking all four tires. Thankfully, they had air. Otherwise, he'd planned to put a real hurt on Wonder Boy. He met Brown a couple of blocks from the residence.

Brown was six feet two inches of football-worthy build. His black hair was cut military short. He didn't say a whole lot, which was fine with Quint.

Quint liked working with Agent Brown, or Brownie, as he'd been nicknamed.

"Hey, Brownie. Are you ready to do this?" Quint asked.

"I've been waiting for you," Brownie quipped as he stood at the driver's-side door of Quint's vehicle.

"I'm guessing you've been watching the place," Quint said.

"The floor plan is a three-bedroom. It's a two-story, and there are cameras. I found the weak spot, though. A bathroom window on the ground floor. Fair warning, it's tiny," Brownie said.

"Why is it always the bathroom window?" Quint groaned.

"They just don't expect us to be able to squeeze through, I guess." Brownie smiled. For a man of his size, Quint heard he could morph his body to fit the smallest places.

"Let's do this." Quint exited his vehicle after firing off a text to Shelly to give her a heads-up. Weapons at the ready and no darkness to shield them, he and Brownie trucked on past a few houses until they'd weaved their way to the bathroom window in question.

"You first," Brownie whispered. "I'll cover out here."

Quint forced the window open. Bathroom window

locks in old houses weren't the hardest to get through. He used Brownie's thigh as leverage to hoist himself up and in. Quint waited for his partner to climb through and join him. They listened at the door of the hall bath to the voices coming from the next room.

"Any chance you speak Romanian?" Quint asked in barely a whisper.

Brownie compressed his lips into a frown as he shook his head.

They could go in guns blazing and risk a bullet with Lili, which seemed like a horrible idea. There was no way Quint could do that to the little girl or her mother. No. They needed a distraction.

The wait seemed like an eternity. But the break came when someone knocked on the front door. A few seconds later, an argument broke out. Baptiste came running down the hall with Lili.

Quint jumped in front of Baptiste, and then threw a knockout punch that dazed the guy, grabbing the little girl before she fell to the floor. Capitalizing on the moment, Brownie made his move. A choke hold that Quint didn't wish on anybody. His respect level for Brownie went up a few more notches, though. The little girl was winding up to belt out a cry. Quint covered her mouth with his hand and tried to get her to make eye contact. No use. She was too young to understand any of this, so he made a funny face at her as Brownie took the man to the ground in a few moves that would make any high school wrestler proud.

When Baptiste was facedown and in cuffs, Quint handed over Lili and went for the living room.

Matias and Constantin were midfight. The door was open, and Wonder Boy rushed in about the same time as Quint. Great.

"Try not to get in my way," Quint shouted to the DEA agent. Shelly was nowhere to be seen, but then, Wonder Boy probably told her to wait in the car so he could take all the credit.

"What are you doing here?" Nick asked.

Quint had no time for small talk. As it was, Constantin had come up with a gun that was presently pointed at Matias's chest. Quint dived at them both and wrestled the gun out of Constantin's hand. The weapon went flying.

"Secure it" was all Quint managed to get out. The DEA agent didn't seem capable of rolling up his sleeves and helping.

Two on one, Quint struggled for control of the fight. He took a couple of punches to the stomach and a kick to the shin that was going to leave a mark. It wasn't until Shelly arrived that he started to get the upper hand. She jumped into the fray as Wonder Boy stood near the door with his phone in hand, texting.

This guy needed to be slapped.

"You got him?" Quint asked Shelly as she rolled on top of Matias, practically crushing his arms, forcing them against his torso.

"I got this," she confirmed through gasps. Sure enough, she wrangled a pair of handcuffs onto Matias and then sat him on his backside.

By then, Quint had Constantin in cuffs.

"Do you plan on actually getting your hands dirty,

Wonder Boy?" Quint probably shouldn't goad Nick, but he couldn't help himself. People like him made the job even more dangerous.

"What did you say?" Nick asked, looking ready to pick a fight now that all the heavy lifting was done. "I'm involving local police if you must know."

"This one belongs to us," Quint reassured.

A scared little girl cried in the background. All Quint could think was that he needed to get her to her mother.

Brownie poked his head in, looking like he didn't know what to do with the screaming kid in his arms.

"Grab the car seat out of the Lambo parked out back. I need to get this baby to her mother," Quint said as he took the little girl from Brownie's arms. "We're going to take you to your momma."

The little angel with big puffy red eyes said, "Momma?"

"That's right. Momma," Quint said. Before he could check his phone to see where Ree was, she came bolting through the door.

The little girl hiccupped as she stuck her thumb in her mouth.

"I got here as fast as I could." Ree turned around and said, "It's done. It's safe. You can come take Lili now."

Ree gave a knowing look to Quint, and he realized Lola must have agreed to testify. She came running into the house as soon as Ree gave the green light, as did Esteban.

"My mother," Lola said as she took her daughter in

her arms and started gently bouncing. "She will join us. No? That is the deal. No?"

"Your mother is being picked up by our agents as we speak." Quint double-checked his phone. "In fact, she's boarding a helicopter that will take her to an airport. She'll be here in the States by morning."

"Thank you," Lola said, hugging her daughter tighter to her chest. "It's been a nightmare ever since I realized what kind of person Matias was. I didn't know, and then I got pregnant. I don't regret my daughter, but I'm so tired of this life."

"And your brother?" Quint asked.

Lola nodded. "Is waiting in the car. He never wanted any part of this. He's a good person. He did what he had to in order to protect Lili."

"You're safe now," Quint reassured. "Let's get you out of here."

Lola nodded.

"You can't leave my scene," Nick stated.

"Don't worry," Shelly said to Quint. "I'll corroborate your side of the story."

"So will I," Brownie confirmed.

"Nick, it's time you took a desk job," Shelly said. "You won't get away with this one."

Quint gave her a quick salute before ushering his witness out the door. Ree followed, staying silent until they made it to the truck. Esteban joined them along the way, and it didn't take twenty minutes for a US marshal to pick up the family.

"Best of luck to you, Lola," Ree said, and in a surprise move gave Lola a hug.

"Thank you. Because of you, she'll have a life," Lola said. "Bless you and your family."

"I don't have a family of my own," Ree corrected.

"Someday, you will. And it will be beautiful," Lola said before walking away with the marshal.

Ree turned to Quint and said, "I guess our work is done."

"I'm not so sure about that," he said. "We'll be in paperwork up to our ears sorting this mess out."

"I'll leave most of that to you," she said. "I'm tired, and I need to sleep in my own bed tonight."

She turned to walk away, but he couldn't let her leave things like that. Not with so much left unsaid.

"Ree," he started.

She stopped.

"What if I'm not ready to be done?" he asked.

"I'm listening," she said.

"How big is your bed?" he asked, hope filling his chest.

"Give me a couple of days and come measure for yourself," she said as she kept walking in the opposite direction.

"I will," he said, and he fully meant it.

* * * * *

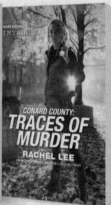

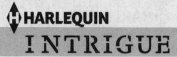
#2079 SHERIFF IN THE SADDLE
The Law in Lubbock County • by Delores Fossen

The town wants her to arrest her former boyfriend, bad boy Cullen Brodie, for a murder on his ranch—but Sheriff Leigh Mercer has no evidence and refuses. The search for the killer draws them passionately close again...and into relentless danger. Not only could Leigh lose her job for not collaring Brodie...but they could both lose their lives.

#2080 ALPHA TRACKER
K-9s on Patrol • by Cindi Myers

After lawman Dillon Diaz spent one incredible weekend with the mysterious Roslyn Kern, he's shocked to encounter her months later when he's assigned to rescue an injured hiker in the mountains. Now, battling a fiery blaze and an escaped fugitive, it's up to Dillon and his K-9, Bentley, to protect long-lost Rosie—and Dillon's unborn child.

#2081 EYEWITNESS MAN AND WIFE
A Ree and Quint Novel • by Barb Han

Relentless ATF agent Quint Casey won't let his best lead die with a murdered perp. He and his undercover wife, Agent Ree Sheppard, must secretly home in on a powerful weapons kingpin. But their undeniable attraction is breaking too many rules for them to play this mission safe—or guarantee their survival...

#2082 CLOSING IN ON THE COWBOY
Kings of Coyote Creek • by Carla Cassidy

Rancher Johnny King thought he'd moved on since Chelsea Black broke their engagement and shattered his heart. But with his emotions still raw following his father's murder, Chelsea's return to town and vulnerability touches Johnny's heart. And when a mysterious stalker threatens Chelsea's life, protecting her means risking his heart again for the woman who abandoned him.

#2083 RETRACING THE INVESTIGATION
The Saving Kelby Creek Series • by Tyler Anne Snell

When Sheriff Jones Murphy rescues his daughter and her teacher, the widower is surprised to encounter Cassandra West again—and there's no mistaking she's pregnant. Now someone wants her dead for unleashing a secret that stunned their town. And though his heart is closed, Jones's sense of duty isn't letting anyone hurt what is his.

#2084 CANYON CRIME SCENE
The Lost Girls • by Carol Ericson

Cade Larson needs LAPD fingerprint expert Lori Del Valle's help tracking down his troubled sister. And when fingerprints link Cade's sister to another missing woman—and a potentially nefarious treatment center—Lori volunteers to go undercover. Will their dangerous plan bring a predator to justice or tragically end their reunion?

Rancher Johnny King thought he'd moved on since Chelsea Black broke their engagement and shattered his heart. But with his emotions still raw following his father's murder, Chelsea's return to town and her vulnerability touches Johnny's heart. And when a mysterious stalker threatens Chelsea's life, protecting her means risking his heart again for the woman who abandoned him.

Read on for a sneak preview of
Closing in on the Cowboy,
the first installment of the
Kings of Coyote Creek miniseries
by New York Times *bestselling author Carla Cassidy!*

"CHELSEA, WHAT'S GOING ON?" Johnny clutched his cell phone to his ear and at the same time he sat up and turned on the lamp on his nightstand.

"That man...that man is here. He tried to b-break in." The words came amid sobs. "He...he was at my back d-door and breaking the gl-glass to get in."

"Hang up and call Lane," he instructed as he got out of bed.

"I...already called, but n-nobody is here yet."

Johnny could hear the abject terror in her voice, and an icy fear shot through him. "Where are you now?"

"I'm in the kitchen."

"Get to the bathroom and lock yourself in. Do you hear me? Lock yourself in the bathroom, and I'll be there as quickly as I can," he instructed.

"Please hurry. I don't know where he is now, and I'm so scared."

"Just get to the bathroom. Lock the door and don't open it for anyone but me or the police." He hung up and quickly dressed. He then strapped on his gun and left his cabin. Any residual sleepiness he might have felt was instantly gone, replaced by a sharp edge of tension that tightened his chest.

Don't miss
Closing in on the Cowboy *by Carla Cassidy,*
available July 2022 wherever
Harlequin Intrigue books and ebooks are sold.

Harlequin.com

HIEXP0522

Get 4 FREE REWARDS!

We'll send you 2 FREE Books plus 2 FREE Mystery Gifts.

FREE
Value Over
$20

Both the **Harlequin Intrigue®** and **Harlequin® Romantic Suspense** series feature compelling novels filled with heart-racing action-packed romance that will keep you on the edge of your seat.

YES! Please send me 2 FREE novels from the Harlequin Intrigue or Harlequin Romantic Suspense series and my 2 FREE gifts (gifts are worth about $10 retail). After receiving them, if I don't wish to receive any more books, I can return the shipping statement marked "cancel." If I don't cancel, I will receive 6 brand-new Harlequin Intrigue Larger-Print books every month and be billed just $5.99 each in the U.S. or $6.49 each in Canada, a savings of at least 14% off the cover price or 4 brand-new Harlequin Romantic Suspense books every month and be billed just $4.99 each in the U.S. or $5.74 each in Canada, a savings of at least 13% off the cover price. It's quite a bargain! Shipping and handling is just 50¢ per book in the U.S. and $1.25 per book in Canada.* I understand that accepting the 2 free books and gifts places me under no obligation to buy anything. I can always return a shipment and cancel at any time. The free books and gifts are mine to keep no matter what I decide.

Choose one: ☐ **Harlequin Intrigue**
Larger-Print
(199/399 HDN GNXC)

☐ **Harlequin Romantic Suspense**
(240/340 HDN GNMZ)

Name (please print)

Address   Apt. #

City   State/Province   Zip/Postal Code

Email: Please check this box ☐ if you would like to receive newsletters and promotional emails from Harlequin Enterprises ULC and its affiliates. You can unsubscribe anytime.

Mail to the **Harlequin Reader Service:**
IN U.S.A.: P.O. Box 1341, Buffalo, NY 14240-8531
IN CANADA: P.O. Box 603, Fort Erie, Ontario L2A 5X3

Want to try 2 free books from another series? Call 1-800-873-8635 or visit www.ReaderService.com.

---

*Terms and prices subject to change without notice. Prices do not include sales taxes, which will be charged (if applicable) based on your state or country of residence. Canadian residents will be charged applicable taxes. Offer not valid in Quebec. This offer is limited to one order per household. Books received may not be as shown. Not valid for current subscribers to the Harlequin Intrigue or Harlequin Romantic Suspense series. All orders subject to approval. Credit or debit balances in a customer's account(s) may be offset by any other outstanding balance owed by or to the customer. Please allow 4 to 6 weeks for delivery. Offer available while quantities last.

Your Privacy—Your information is being collected by Harlequin Enterprises ULC, operating as Harlequin Reader Service. For a complete summary of the information we collect, how we use this information and to whom it is disclosed, please visit our privacy notice located at corporate.harlequin.com/privacy-notice. From time to time we may also exchange your personal information with reputable third parties. If you wish to opt out of this sharing of your personal information, please visit readerservice.com/consumerchoice or call 1-800-873-8635. **Notice to California Residents**—Under California law, you have specific rights to control and access your data. For more information on these rights and how to exercise them, visit corporate.harlequin.com/california-privacy.

HIHRS22

Love Harlequin romance?

DISCOVER.

Be the first to find out about promotions,
news and exclusive content!

Facebook.com/HarlequinBooks

Twitter.com/HarlequinBooks

Instagram.com/HarlequinBooks

Pinterest.com/HarlequinBooks

YouTube.com/HarlequinBooks

ReaderService.com

EXPLORE.

Sign up for the Harlequin e-newsletter and
download a free book from any series at
TryHarlequin.com

CONNECT.

Join our Harlequin community to
share your thoughts and connect
with other romance readers!
Facebook.com/groups/HarlequinConnection